WHEN IT POURS

Rachel Pluck

ISBN-13: 979-8-9926024-1-1

For my amazing mother, Joy.
Thank you for showing me what strength looks like.

CHapTer 1

Cate

IF I COULD TACKLE Paul Andrews right now without getting fired, I would.

He'd go down easy, I think. He's tall, but built more like a beanpole than a brick wall. I'd have the element of surprise on my side. He'd never see my right shoulder coming until it's too late, when it's already connected with his ribcage.

That flawless white shirt of his would be full of wrinkles when I'm done. He'd probably be more horrified by that than anything.

While he finishes walking through last month's profit and loss statement, I let the fantasy play over and over in my head, trying not to smile. A smile would give me away; I rarely smile during budget meetings. I have even less reason to smile in this one.

Paul's forearms are braced against the long glass table we're all seated around, his attention focused on his open laptop. He didn't even have the decency to look up from his spreadsheets when he called me out in front of the entire VitaPop staff. When the blue-painted walls of this conference room began to close in on me.

I used to love the color blue—how it's proven to help with concentration and relaxation. Now it will only remind me of this meeting.

On the outside, I keep my lips pressed into a thin line, my chin held high. I can't let everyone know I'm mortified by the way Paul *so thoughtfully* offered his (unsolicited) advice on a few digital marketing campaigns I could "just cut" because they weren't performing "up to standards."

Like he even knows what our performance standards are! Like saving a few bucks now will somehow make thousands of people go out and buy our company's prebiotic sodas. Like the blame for the company not hitting its sales goal last month rests squarely on my shoulders.

Like he couldn't have simply approached me in private to ask about my work before calling me out in an all-hands meeting!

Hence my violent fantasy.

I cock my head to the side and gaze through the lone window in this conference room, completely tuned out at this point. The two-lane road outside our corporate campus is busy, other office workers heading out for lunch, most likely. Lucky them.

Letting out a slow exhale through my nose, I try to focus on what's happening in the room around me. Paul's droning on about some software charge that showed up unexpectedly on a billing statement, I think?

Who cares?

Against my will, my mind wanders back to the one thing I'm trying to forget. Sure, I may have taken a risk on a few new campaigns last month that aren't converting as quickly as we're used to, but it's worth it. It will be. Those new ads will bring in five times their cost... eventually.

Besides, marketing is only one small piece of the pie. Or "one ingredient on the VitaPop nutrition label!" as Darius likes to say.

Thank god for my boss. When Paul first called me out, I'd gone white as a sheet. I never knew what it meant before, when books said the color drained from someone's face, until it happened to me. Places on my body that have never sweat before got clammy. My gut churned like I had a bad hangover.

Darius had smiled politely back at Paul and tipped his head. "Thank you for your input, Paul. We'll take it under consideration." I'd blanched at that, hands balling into fists against my thighs. Then Darius shot me a quick wink no one else would notice and I could breathe again.

Of course he wouldn't take Paul seriously. Darius knows me. Trusts me. He's smarter than that.

I haven't felt this personally attacked since the VitaPop Ugly Christmas Sweater soiree two years ago. Paul took one look at my homemade sweater, its blinking lights and tinsel draped every which way, and said, "Gunning for that top prize today, huh?" And then he just walked away.

I guess he's graduated from personal gibes to full on job performance assaults now.

Geez, is this guy still talking?

His voice is like the drone of a robot in an old eighties film. Deep in a way that could be pleasant if it wasn't also drier than desert sand.

I shift in my seat, uncrossing and recrossing my legs to keep them from falling asleep in my uncomfortable-but-chic, curved, low-back chair. If only I could do the same thing to my brain. The movement flashes a sliver of once-pale skin, now tinged the color of a plum, on my right thigh. It peeks out from beneath my corduroy skirt for a second, like it's waving hello, before it's hidden away again.

Not the first time I took a ball to the leg at rugby practice, and it certainly won't be the last.

"That about wraps things up for today. Thank you all for your time." I'm not sure when Darius cut in to end the meeting and I startle in my seat, searching his body language for anything important I may have missed. Too late. The stuffy room comes alive, everyone shuffling papers and pens or closing their laptops, eager to escape and get something to eat.

I join them, snapping up my belongings in a frenzy to be one of the first people out of the overheated room.

"That was awkward," my coworker Mindy says to me when we get back to our cubicle. We've sat directly across a narrow aisle from one another since I started here at VitaPop three years ago. We've lived together in a small, weathered house in Seattle's Arbor Heights neighborhood for just over one of those years.

And right now, she's only partially right.

Awkward is putting it mildly. Awkward is when you accidentally misspell someone's name in an email. Awkward is when you lean too far back in one of the space-age chairs in the conference room and nearly topple backwards.

What happened in that room today wasn't awkward. It was Paul Freaking Andrews.

Accountant.

Archenemy.

Hater of Marketing.

Probable murderer of puppies.

"Paul Freaking Andrews," I hiss under my breath without realizing it, stabbing my index finger against my keyboard a little too forcefully to wake up my laptop.

"What?" Mindy asks, swiveling halfway around in her chair to glance at me, one jet-black eyebrow raised.

I cough to play it off and enter my password. "Nothing, sorry. Talking to myself."

"Practicing your pitch again?" she teases, following my lead and pulling up a file for a print ad she's working on for yours truly. Not even halfway done and it already looks amazing. She truly is a gifted graphic designer.

I smile at my screen, some of the anger burning off. "No more practice needed. I've got it in the bag." Darius is going to love my proposal for the new soda launch, I'm certain. And by this time next year, I'll have a shiny new ornament for my desk—my very own Edie Award for the Best Influencer Marketing Campaign in the mid-size company division. Anyone who's anyone in marketing has one of these awards—the best of the best. And this time next year, I'll be one of them.

Its twin will be back home in Pueblito del Sol, California, on the polished wood shelf in my parents' den, standing a little bit taller than my older brother's high school football trophies, a lot shinier than my little sister's cheerleading ribbons. My own place among my siblings, finally.

Mindy smiles slyly and wiggles her eyebrows at me. "Get it, girl. You bring lunch today?" She already knows the answer, but I love her for asking anyway.

"Yep, today it's—"

"Don't tell me: soup?"

I return her sly smile over my shoulder. "Not just any soup, pasta e fagioli." My absolute favorite. Every Sunday, when Mindy goes to her parents' house for family dinner, I make a giant batch of soup to set myself up with lunch for the week. I make this one at least once a month, but usually more.

"Enjoy," she teases, already locking her computer screen to head out for a bite.

I pull up the slide deck for the presentation I'm giving in two days. Mindy helped me with the layout and visuals, but the flow and copy is all me. It's perfect. Crisp, clear, the right amount of bold and disruptive, with a splash of fun.

I've been through it about three dozen times. I can deliver it in my sleep.

My stomach growls when I reach the last slide—for the three-dozen-and-first time—and I pat a hand against it. After clearing and locking my screen, I rise to grab my lunch from the fridge.

The small office kitchen is adjacent to where Mindy and I sit, walled off to (kind of) keep the smells of the microwave at bay, and accessible by a single door. Right now it's empty. Most employees prefer to either eat at their desk, like me, or venture off campus for their allotted hour, like Mindy.

The fridge door closes with a small thud and, when I turn around to face the microwave, I realize I was wrong. There is one other person in the room.

Paul Andrews.

He sits opposite where I stand, at the large center island that pulls double duty as both a food prep station and a bar-height seating area. We lock eyes for a long moment over his sandwich, him pausing mid-chew. *It's probably ham*, I think for some reason. He probably eats a ham sandwich every day. Plain, like him. No mayo or mustard. Because they have too many calories, or they're too flavorful, or some other reason that makes no sense.

After what I know has been too long, he gives me a small nod that ruffles his sandy blond hair, then drops eye contact. I shove my glass container full of goodness into the microwave and set it for two minutes.

The two of us trying to ignore one another is like a third presence in the room, sucking all the air out of the place. I look at the colorful mural on the wall behind him. I look at the plain white ceiling overhead, a splatter of something that was once red marring its otherwise pristine surface. I look at the time on the microwave, which tells me only thirty seconds have passed.

I fight the urge to groan my impatience out loud.

Without meaning to, I look at Paul Andrews. Though it physically pains me to admit it, worse than when I got the bruise on my leg at practice two days ago, he wouldn't be so plain if he didn't wear the same starchy, white button down and khaki pants every single day. Or if he smiled a little.

His jawline is sharp, even when he chews. From this angle, I can see the tops of his dark blue irises, his eyes cast down at the table like he can decipher secret messages in the wood grain if he tries hard enough. I smile a little to myself, taking small relief in the fact that he's as uncomfortable as I am.

I can't help but wonder if he feels bad for throwing me under the bus in the staff meeting or if he simply enjoys being evil for no reason. What have I ever done to him? I always turn in my expense reports on time. I've never gone over budget without getting approval first.

I don't get it.

Maybe it's just me he doesn't like. Wouldn't be the first time.

Between bites, he takes a deep breath that shifts the stiff collar of his shirt, opening it a bit farther at the top—the only button left undone. There's a nick beside the hollow of his throat, his only imperfection. A shaving injury, perhaps?

The microwave beeps too loudly in the quiet space, making both of us jump. Collecting my soup as quickly as I can, I nearly sprint for the door.

It's not hot enough, I can already tell. I usually need to stir it and put it back in for another thirty seconds or so, but I can't stand being alone in that kitchen with him for one moment longer.

CHAPTER 2

Paul

SHE'S GIVING ME THAT look again.

The one where her mouth twists to one side, upper lip on the verge of curling, her left eyebrow arching in unspoken question. I can feel the prick of her eyes against my skin, like little mosquito bites.

This look, she seems to reserve it for only me. Everyone else gets a beaming smile or bright round eyes or an encouraging nod. I've only ever seen her use this look with one other person, and I'm not even sure who it was. She'd been on the phone, pacing outside of our office building one day when I was trying to leave, speaking in terse, hushed whispers. That was almost two years ago.

I remember because she'd been wearing the craziest Christmas sweater I've ever seen. Covered in lights and garland and plenty of other knickknacks. I'm pretty sure she made it herself. It was kind of impressive. I tried to tell her as much, but she gave me a weird look—*this look*—and I ran away from it. She must have something against compliments. Or maybe she has something against me.

I keep my eyes carefully trained on the table, counting exactly twenty-five chews for every bite before swallowing. When the microwave finally beeps, I have to resist the urge to sprint from the table, leaving my half-eaten sandwich and strawberry soda—courtesy of the well-stocked VitaPop fridge—abandoned.

In reality, I sit perfectly still in the way I've perfected over the past ten years. I lift only my eyes, and only when I'm sure she's gathered her lunch—some kind of red soup from the look of it—and breezed through the door, leaving nothing but the faint scent of tomato sauce and peonies behind.

Alone again, I sigh into my sandwich.

I'm pretty sure the glare she gave me has something to do with the staff meeting. She'd barely spoken, which is unusual for her. Normally she hangs around at the end for small talk. Not with me, obviously, but with the others. Today she'd run out of the room like her life depended on it.

I don't usually present the profit and loss report in these meetings, but my boss is out of town for two weeks and needed me to fill in. If I didn't know any better, I'd say he planned it. The numbers I had to share were... not great.

Sales were down last month for the first time in half a year, and I was the lucky guy who got to tell everyone. To let the team down. I spent the better part of last week preparing (read: panicking), trying to find something positive to share instead.

Logically, I know a drop in sales isn't any one person's fault. Especially not an accountant's. Still, I wanted a silver lining. More importantly, I wanted something to take the spotlight off of me.

When I read Cate's reports last week and saw those two campaigns were bleeding money, it seemed like the perfect thing to share. The company would save money. Cate's department would save money. Or spend it on something else, I don't care. That's her job to figure out. I thought she'd be pleased, or at least interested in talking more about it.

Instead she'd looked like I'd stabbed her with a dull spoon.

There was a time in my life when I was like her. So sure of myself. That all my ideas were right. That every risk I took, no matter how costly, was worth it. That I could take on the world, make anything happen, by sheer force of will alone.

It's a luxury I can't afford now.

She'll learn it herself soon enough, like I did. For her sake, I hope the lesson comes easier. I snort without humor and ball up the sheet of foil—all that's left of my sandwich—I've been using as a plate and toss it into the trash.

I'm back in my sparsely-appointed office—apparently being one of only two accountants in the company affords me one—for only a few minutes before Darius pokes his head through the open door and raps twice on the frame. "Got a sec?"

There's something sage about him. Someone who's been around, seen a few things, and now possesses the ethereal sort of wisdom that can't be learned in a classroom. I don't know what the Director of Commercial Planning is supposed to do, but he seems to do it well nonetheless. I find myself straightening the pens and papers dotting my desk, nodding eagerly in his direction until he steps inside and shuts my door.

Darius makes himself comfortable in the lone chair across from me, casually crossing an ankle over the opposite knee. "I need to loop you into a meeting on Wednesday," he says without preamble, another reason why I've always liked him.

On the surface, his request is unsurprising. Often, my boss finds himself yanked into chats, email threads, and even scheduled discussions. The ones most people hope can happen without Accounting's input but almost always require it. If we're being smart.

Sometimes I get dragged right along with him. It's fine, I love helping. Only, it seems like we're the bearers of bad news more often than not.

This would be my first time flying solo, though. It feels like an opportunity and a trap all in one. I clear my throat, back going stick-straight, and pull up my calendar. "Sure thing."

"Cate's presenting a campaign idea for the new soda launch." This time, Darius's voice is noticeably quieter.

My hand freezes mid-click. *Oh no.*

"I know whatever she's got will be great, but..."

I roll my lips into a thin line and force myself to look at the man across from me, noticing for the first time the tiniest flush across his cheeks. After releasing a silent sigh through my nose, I finish for him, "But you want to make sure it's financially feasible before agreeing to anything."

Darius nods, sheepish.

The urge to fulfill a stereotype and pinch the bridge of my nose between my thumb and index finger becomes almost unbearable.

They should change our department title to Company Attack Dogs.

Crushers of Dreams.

The Executioners.

Why break the bad news about the budget yourself when you can have Accounting do it? Not enough profit for big Christmas bonuses this year? Accounting can explain why. Can't afford the campaign idea someone's spent months working on? No problem, ask Accounting to shut it down.

Swallowing the thoughts, I nod, and Darius grins. "I'll send you an invite, thanks man!"

I nod again as he stands, because what else can I do, and watch him walk out. My mind drifts to Cate, the way she'd looked at me during the staff meeting this morning. Like one of the lions in the nature shows my dad loves. Right before it takes down an antelope, maw clamped tight over the jugular.

I hope Darius tells her I'll be there.

CHAPTER 3

Cate

I CAN'T BELIEVE DARIUS didn't warn me he'd invited Paul Freaking Andrews to my pitch. I take back every nice thing I thought about him on Monday.

Okay, maybe not everything. In every other way, he's kind of a great boss. But inviting my archnemesis to the most important pitch of my life? Come on!

Paul was already sitting in the conference room when we'd walked in, laptop open in front of him, hands folded against the table. Probably shows up five minutes early to every meeting, scoping out the best seat, asserting his dominance like a king from a throne.

"Great, you're already here!" Darius chirps, grabbing a seat across from Paul like it's nothing.

I eye the only remaining open seats with a disdain I haven't felt since my little sister borrowed my favorite pair of Ugg boots in high school and then spilled a mocha frappuccino all over them. Usually, I'd sit across from Darius for this kind of thing. Casual.

But that would mean I'd have to sit beside Paul, which feels entirely unacceptable.

Both men finally look up to where I stand frozen in the doorway. Darius wears an encouraging smile. Paul wears a completely unreadable look that makes me feel like a toddler who's just been reprimanded for coloring on the walls.

I cough into my elbow, a weak pass at an excuse for stalling, and march with sure footing to the front of the room. If they're going to give me an audience, then I'm going to give them a show.

When my slide deck fills the screen behind me, I dive in. Paul's presence unnerves me and I stumble a few times over my opening lines. He doesn't look at me once, but I can feel his attention as sure as a weight on my chest. Listening to each and every word, looking for ways to twist them back on me, no doubt.

Darius is oblivious, of course. If he senses I'm off my game, he doesn't show it. His eyes are bright with interest, glued to me and the visuals at my back while I walk through the slides, the gears in his head turning with every possibility they propose.

In two months, VitaPop will release a brand-new soda flavor: CitraCrush, our take on an orange crush minus the alcohol and with added antioxidants and prebiotics. In the lead-up to the release, I propose our largest-scale social media influencer campaign yet: partnerships with ten of the most revered voices in the consumer lifestyle space today. One influencer for each of VitaPop's nine existing soda flavors, culminating with the queen herself, Lauren Roth, who will personally reveal CitraCrush to her ten million followers and the world.

It's smart, it's relevant, it's exactly what we need to take VitaPop from the fringe to a household name.

With that mantra chanting in my mind, I manage to pull it together for the last few slides. The quiver disappears from my voice and my hand no longer shakes where it hovers over my computer's trackpad.

By the time I finish, my heart rate is still a little elevated, my breaths heaving like I'm going for a pacy walk, but my smile is wide.

And so is Darius's. He nodded at all the right moments, laughed right on cue for one of Mindy's hilarious visual animations. He loves it, I can already tell. I lean against the edge of the conference room table and open my mouth to speak.

Darius beats me to the punch. "What do you think, Paul?"

My eyebrows shoot up on my forehead, jaw going slack. He can't be serious. Who cares what Paul thinks? He wouldn't know a good marketing idea if it bit him in the ass.

"I think." Paul clears his throat, his eyes focused on his computer screen. For the first time, I look his way and notice he has a copy of my slide deck pulled up. He's staring at the last slide, my cost projections. My stomach sinks.

"I think," he starts again, then stops to rub his chin with his thumb and forefinger. Finally, he leans back in his chair and drops his hands to his lap, folded like a schoolboy's. "We can't afford it."

Those four words suck the air from my lungs. I'm surprised I don't wilt right there like an unwatered flower.

Paul at least has the good sense not to look at me, his eyes instead lifting to Darius. "Not all of it, anyway."

Oh good, so he wants to chop my brilliant idea up, auction it off for parts. What a comfort.

I am dumbfounded when Darius grins. "That sounds like the start of a fun challenge." *A fun challenge? Have you completely lost your mind?*

For the first time in the history of forever, Paul and I wear mirror expressions: lips parted, forehead wrinkled in the center, eyebrows low over our eyes. We stare expectantly across the table at Darius, waiting for him to explain.

He looks between the two of us, his grin going crooked. I think he even has the audacity to chuckle. Chuckle! At a time like this!

"Cate," he begins, facing me first, and I do my best to lift my chin. "This idea is brilliant." I smile. *Maybe this won't be so bad after all.* Darius's eyes flick to my left. "But Paul's right, we don't have the budget for it." And just like that, my smile is gone again.

If he had told me the budget cap upfront, one of the *six times* I'd asked him, maybe I could've pivoted. But noooo, he said he didn't want to stifle my creativity. To pen my ideas in a box.

Well, what does he think he's doing now?

"Darius, I think this could be a huge opportunity for the brand," I manage to stammer, not ready to give up.

His eyes flick back to me. "I agree, which is why I'd like you to find a way to make it work. Something like it, anyway." He pauses, and I'm ninety-nine percent sure it's for dramatic effect, which makes me simultaneously enraged and impressed in equal measure. "Both of you. Together."

CHAPTER 4

Paul

I TAKE BACK EVERYTHING I thought on Monday about Darius and his sage wisdom. He has clearly lost it, or maybe he never even had it. Simply a great actor, faking his way until he makes it.

It was bad enough that he didn't even bother to tell Cate I would be here today. That much was clear by the look of absolute shock, and possibly mild disgust, on her face when she walked in.

Now this?

There is no way this will work.

Darius looks to Cate. "This is the perfect opportunity for us to collaborate. Develop the campaign of our dreams." He turns to me. "And do it smart."

I open and close my mouth a few times like a fish, trying to come up with something to say other than "This is the worst idea in the history of ideas." Something tells me even infinitely-kind Darius has his limits, and I don't even want to imagine what my boss would say if that got back to him.

Fortunately, Cate speaks for me. "I don't think I'm following, what are you asking us to do?" Did I imagine that she choked on the word *us*? Literally choked.

Darius leans forward, gesturing to each of us with an upturned palm. "I want the two of you to work together. Tweak the proposal until it's something game-changing *and* affordable."

Frustration is radiating off of Cate in waves and she's giving that look—*my* look—to the blue-painted walls. I resist the urge to smile bitterly.

I knew this would happen.

Okay, I didn't know Darius would lose his ever-loving mind and try to team me up with Cate to work on a... marketing campaign. Not even M. Night Shyamalan could have written that plot twist.

I did have a feeling I'd be playing the role of the bad guy in this meeting. Still, it hurt to make the words come out when the time came. I didn't want to ruin her idea.

From what little I know about marketing, it seemed to have merit.

I tried. I stared at that screen and willed the numbers to add up to something else. They couldn't. Math doesn't work that way; it's black and white and sometimes red. The thing I love about it so much has doomed me.

So I did my job and crushed her dreams and figured that would be the end of it.

Instead, Darius says, "I know we're in a bit of a time crunch here, but can you have another proposal together in the next week?"

Not sure what else to do, I look to Cate. Her pink lips are twisted to one side, a little rosebud, as she considers. I wonder if the soft petals hide thorns, then force myself to stop staring at her mouth. Just in time, too. She points her hazel eyes to me and her chest rises and falls in a deep breath. I have to blink to keep from tracking the movement.

"Okay," she says after another breath, and I can't stop the look of surprise that flits across my face.

"Excellent!" Darius cheers. The thunderclap of his palms meeting echoes through the close quarters. He tucks his laptop under his arm and rises to cross the room. "I'll leave you two to it."

Seconds pass while neither Cate nor I move, both of us staring straight ahead. When I can't take it any longer, I turn in my chair until my knees are pointed in her direction. "Should we—"

"I'm sorry, I didn't realize what time it was. I have to hop on a call," Cate cuts me off, her movements robotic as she stands and pulls her computer to her chest. She doesn't even spare me a passing glance on her way out the door, yelling over her shoulder, "Let's connect later!"

"Right," I grumble under my breath when she's already long gone.

CHAPTER 5

Cate

SWEAT BEADS ALONG MY brow and drips down the side of my neck, but the cool relief it leaves behind is fleeting. The song changes and Chappell Roan's "Femininomenon" plays from the speaker in the corner at a volume that is not quite as loud as I'd like it to be. I press the up button on the treadmill five times to increase my speed to a sprint.

I try to time my steps—at least two long strides per inhale and another two per exhale—but I'm almost forty minutes in and running has never been my strong suit. *One more song*, I tell myself, *then you're done*. I pump my arms harder to maintain my pace, determined to see the odometer reach four miles.

"It's not just about speed, Seymour," my coach told me last week at practice. "Even short runs require stamina."

Chappell stops singing and Mindy beside me is already cooling down, but I take eight more long strides and pump my fist once in front of my chest when that little number behind the decimal rolls over to zero one final time. Sweat drips across my smile.

"Was that a PR?" Mindy asks, wiping her brow with one of the white towels they keep stocked in the campus gym. They're soft but they always smell like bleach, despite the spring fresh fabric softener they use.

I don't mind it, though. Bleach means clean, even if it stings my nostrils when I accidentally inhale while scrubbing one across my face.

It takes me about a minute to catch my breath enough to answer her. "Yep, beat my last time by forty seconds." I wiggle my eyebrows at her then take a deep swig from my water bottle.

She pretends to bow at the waist, fanning me with outstretched arms, and I shake my head while powering down my treadmill. "Maybe I should join your rugby team, if it'll give me gains like that." She gestures with her chin toward my curled arm, my bicep bulging a little as I wipe the sweat from my neck.

"My offer still stands," I sing-song, draping the damp towel around my shoulders. I know she's kidding, but it doesn't stop me from asking. Again.

"Yeah right," she says, blowing a breath that makes her lips puff out and smack together noisily. "You know I can't take a hit. I'd be on the ground sobbing after my first tackle."

Shrugging, I catch my right ankle in my hand, folding into a quad stretch. The tackling part never bothered me. Sure, I don't actively want to get knocked to the ground; no one does. It's part of the game, and I'm fortunate this sport prioritizes doing it as safely as possible. Injuries still happen, but it's better than it could be.

Besides, you don't get taken out unless you're vital to the game. A tackle means you're doing something right. It's a badge of honor.

"Speaking of tackling, have you talked to Paul about your project yet?"

I groan loudly and drop my ankle, then pick up the other in the same stretch. "Don't remind me."

"I'll take that as a *no*," Mindy mocks, stepping back into a modified lunge. "You can't avoid it forever, you know."

"It's been two days, Min. I'm not avoiding, I've just been extremely busy." As has she. We both got pulled into a last-minute request to revamp some of our brochures before a trade show next month. It was all hands on deck yesterday, and I was only too happy for the distraction.

"Two days too many, if you ask me," she answers, switching legs. "You only have a week to figure this out. Suck it up and meet with him."

I groan again, hanging my head back on my shoulders. I've *tried*. So many times, my mouse has hovered over his name in the company chat, but I could never bring myself to click it. Something about being the first to cave makes me break out in hives.

Mindy stops stretching and turns to face me, leaning one slim hip against the front of the treadmill. "It probably won't be that bad."

I mirror her position and arch an eyebrow at her. "It will be terrible. Worse than I can imagine." Lifting my right hand, I start ticking off fingers. "First of all, he's boring. He's not going to understand my vision for the CitraCrush campaign. All he cares about is profit."

"We do work for a business, Cate," Mindy cuts in, and I shoot her a death glare that has her exposing her palms defensively.

"Second of all," I say, ticking off another finger. "He's mean."

Mindy furrows her brows. "He is not *mean*."

"He's blunt."

"*You're* blunt."

I pinch my lips together, considering. She's not wrong. I've had to rein in my own directness more than a few times since I started here. The few times I forgot to do so have haunted me ever since.

"We don't vibe. He's had it out to get me since I started. You saw him in the meeting on Monday. He was only too happy to cut me down. Cut my work down."

Not to mention, this partnership is a little insulting. I'm not against collaboration, but that's not what this feels like. This feels like a leash. More than that, it feels like a lack of trust. *The marketer can't get it right on her own, bring in the finance guy.*

Mindy rolls her lips into her mouth then shrugs. "Maybe you're right. Maybe you're not. Maybe things will be different if you're working on the same side, for the same goal."

I open my mouth to protest, but she stops me with a lifted finger. "Either way, you can't avoid it. Darius put you both on this. Your job depends on it. Time to suck it up." She hops off the treadmill and I follow suit, trailing her to the women's locker room. "Think of it like your biggest challenge yet. One small hill to climb on your road to marketing greatness." She traces the pattern of a rainbow in the air with a wave of her hand and I stifle my snort.

The truth is, it's not just my deeply ingrained loathing of the accountant that has me stalling. Or the disappointment from all but failing miserably in that pitch meeting after I thought I'd had it in the bag.

I genuinely don't know what good it's going to do, us working together. Even if I liked the guy, the proposal I shared was it. My big idea. The campaign that was going to put VitaPop on the map, secure enough attention (and hopefully sales) so my marketing budget would never be questioned again. The one that was going to earn me an Edie Award.

And now it's over.

Darius may have said it nicely, may have given me this other chance, but at the end of the day he shot down my pitch. Sure, it wasn't because he didn't believe in it. I should take some comfort in that. I wish I could.

As much as people like to think of Paul as a wizard with numbers, he's no magician. Unless he can pull an extra fifty thousand dollars out of a hat, there's no point to us working together. We'd meet, maybe stare awkwardly at one another until we decide to move on and never speak of it again. It's almost laughable, if it wasn't my career on the line.

What's that saying? When it rains, it pours.

More like *when it pours, it pours harder.*

When Mindy and I reach the door to the women's locker room, the one beside it opens, startling us both a half-step backwards. The universe must be mocking me, because out walks Paul Andrews, wearing a pair of black athletic shorts and a black, form-fitting T-shirt that hints at lean muscle beneath it.

"Cate. Mindy. Good morning," he says, voice raspy like he just woke up.

Mindy slinks behind him, moving closer to freedom, and widens her eyes at me from behind his back. A grimace stretches her lips wide. I already know what she's wondering, because it's the same question I have: *Did he hear us talking?*

Avoiding eye contact with both of them, I nod, trying to look as unbothered as possible. "Good morning."

In a rush to slip away, I sidestep to the left, but he matches my movement and our feet nearly collide. When I repeat the motion on the right, there he is again. We're performing the most uncomfortable dance ever, our steps growing more erratic and desperate every time we try unsuccessfully to get away from each other.

Finally, we both stop, eyes widened in horror, and wait. When I'm sure it's safe, I take one large step to the right—his left—and safely make it to Mindy and the locker room door. Relief floods my veins and I slap a palm against the heavy wood to push it open.

"Have a good workout," Mindy calls back as she follows me inside, and I can hear the laugh in her voice. I give her a wild look when we're finally safe behind the closed door.

"What? I'm not the one who hates him, remember?"

CHAPTER 6

Paul

So, she thinks I'm boring.

That's no surprise. If anything, I expected worse when I walked into the office gym at seven this morning—thirty minutes earlier than I usually do, because my father was expecting a call from me at eight—and heard her voice bouncing against the high ceilings.

It was one of the last things I'd heard before I quickly realized they were talking about me and ducked into the men's locker room to hide. I'd waited in there for a good ten minutes, praying they'd be long gone by the time I reemerged. My timing had never been so off.

Now, staring at a document of my own design with VitaPop's income and cash flow statements arranged like sheet music, I replay the snippet of conversation I overheard again.

"Boring and bad vibes," or something along those lines, she had said. Whatever that means, coming from a girl who hardly knows me. Who never bothered to try to know me.

That'll be the last time I change up my morning routine. A five-minute check-in with dad while he commutes to his job as a portfolio manager is hardly worth the insult.

I groan at my computer screen, trying to make sense of the numbers that usually speak to me but are being drowned out by a silly blonde girl handing down judgment in a frivolous purple sports bra and matching spandex shorts. This assignment will be impossible. Cate and I haven't spoken more than two words to each other since the meeting with Darius on Wednesday. It's now Friday, and there's still no end to our stalemate in sight.

If she thinks I'll make the first move, she's sorely mistaken. This isn't my project. I'm here as a consultant, if anything. Consultants can't answer questions they've never been asked. My job isn't on the line here, right? It's not like I'm the one who reports to Darius.

Nope, I'll sit here and comb through these financial statements like I always do. If I can get them to—I squint at the screen, trying to focus my thoughts. When my phone vibrates next to my mousepad, I'm only too eager to check the notification, grabbing for it like it might disappear if I don't make contact.

Distracted. I'm distracted. I don't get *distracted*.

My stomach drops when I bring the small screen into focus. I stare at the message preview there until it goes dark again. An invitation. A memorial. Ten-year anniversary. Jake.

Has it really been ten years?

The blood rushing in my ears sounds like a swift-moving river and suddenly I'm back there on that ridge, the scent of moss and dried pine needles filling my nose. Just the two of us, squeezing between the tall trees, feeling safe within their cushion. How wrong we'd been.

I gulp back the dryness in my throat and shake my head to clear the memories then set my phone back on my desk, face down. That's not my life anymore. My eyes lift to the financial statements on my computer screen. This is my life now.

I bite the inside of my cheek and look through the glass wall of my office to the cubicles all the way at the back. Like it or not, I need to see this project through if I want to keep things the way they are. Slipping a hand into my laptop bag, I produce a bottle of aspirin and pop two into my mouth, warding off the headache I know is coming. Then I stand.

Cate pretends not to notice me when I reach her desk, too enthralled with whatever's on her oversized monitor, so I clear my throat. Twice.

It's the first time I've ever popped by her desk and I can't help but snoop a little. It's crawling with little potted plants, a lot of succulents and a viny one spilling out of its planter to trail down the side of her filing cabinet. I think it might be a philodendron of some kind. My mom used to keep them in the house. Maybe she still does. I can't remember if I saw any the last time I visited. Christmas, nearly a year ago.

If I sat at a desk like this for eight hours a day, I'd probably break out in hives from the overstimulation alone. There are little pops of color everywhere I turn: hot pink sticky note pads, a large mushroom figurine made of violet mirrored glass, and a little crochet—wait, is that a dumpster fire? It's holding a little sign that reads "Everything is fine."

Ha, cute, I think and then blanch.

"Cate," I say finally, acute pressure already building between my brows. Should've taken the aspirin earlier.

She blinks up at me slowly, acting surprised to see me there, and I have to lock my eyes into place to stop them from rolling. If she moonlights as an actress, she'd better keep her day job. She's not fooling anyone. "Paul, to what do I owe the pleasure?"

A sharp inhale through my nose, an audible exhale. "When would be a convenient time to meet." There's no inflection at the end of my sentence, so it doesn't sound like a question.

"About?" Her voice flicks up at the end, feigned innocence.

I grind my teeth together until it's almost painful then force my jaw to relax. "The campaign. For the product launch. The one Darius asked"—*forced*— "us to partner on?" There's the inflection I was looking for, but it comes out haughty. A British guy sneering in a period drama.

Cate has the gall to act like this is a new revelation, slow understanding rolling across her expression in a tidal wave. Maybe I was wrong about the acting job. At least then I'd never have to deal with her. "Ah, right." She turns back to her computer, pretends to look at her Outlook calendar. "I'll send you an invite." The way things have been going so far, I get the impression she most certainly will not send me an invite.

By this time, I'm thoroughly annoyed and the pressure in the center of my forehead has built to a crescendo. I slam my palms on her desk a little harder than I mean to and lean forward on bent arms until our heads are a foot apart. This draws her attention. At least now she has the good sense to look intrigued, if a little unsure, one perfectly groomed blonde eyebrow ticked up like an accent symbol.

"Like it or not, we need to work together on this. The sooner we get started, the sooner we can wrap it up. Come to my office at two, we'll hash out logistics then."

Cate's throat works as she swallows, her lower lip jutting out like she wants to say something. Whatever it is, she decides against it, simply nodding her response.

I nod back, sealing the deal, then remove my hands from her desk and my body from her cubicle, holding my head a little bit higher on the walk back to my office. The numbers in my spreadsheet welcome me back with open arms.

The confidence I'd felt this morning, charging over to Cate's desk, has fully waned by the time the little clock on the right-hand corner of my monitor reads 1:55. I can't stop staring at it, almost wishing it were an analog so I could at least watch the minute hand slowly crawl away from and back toward the number twelve over and over again. Anything other than sitting here, pretending to work, while my entire body seems keyed to the open doorway to my office.

She'll probably be late, her way of punishing me for my earlier display. My cheeks flush every time I think about it. Thankfully the designer hadn't been at her desk across the aisle and my parents taught me the value of being a low talker from a young age. I'm pretty sure no one else heard me.

Cate surprises me in the doorway, a whole two minutes early. For some reason, it feels like a trap. I freeze, fighting the urge to rearrange my desk for the third time today. A nervous tick.

She hesitates at the threshold, our unblinking eyes locked, and then steps inside. The scent of peonies wafts in with her, warm and inviting, and I hold my breath to keep from inhaling it deep into my lungs.

"Now still a good time?" she asks formally, folding herself into the only spare chair in here. A rhetorical question to break the ice, but I find myself appreciating it nonetheless. It does something to unfreeze my cramped muscles, relax my spine.

"Of course." I grab for the legal pad and pen I keep beside my computer and slide up to the section of my L-shaped desk that faces her. Pen poised over paper, I stop, knitting my eyebrows. Slowly, I look up at her from beneath them, chin still pointed down so she can see only half my face.

I have no idea how to start this meeting. Cate looks as lost as I feel, one foot tapping nervously where it's crossed over the opposite leg. Wonderful.

"The campaign," I start, hoping I won't have to go any further. That she'll jump in, fill the gap. Maybe I should have reviewed her slide deck again before this. I can't remember the last time I felt so unprepared, exposed.

The silence hanging over us is a thundercloud. Cate's hazel eyes pierce me in the heart then stab tiny daggers against my face. The seconds drag on into hours, months, years. When one corner of her mouth ticks up like it was tugged by a hook, I realize she's perfectly content to watch me flounder like this all day. My nostrils flare and I cough into my hand to hide it.

Finally, she comes to my rescue. "I won't bore you with the details again, but the overall idea was to lean on multiple influencer partnerships in the lead up to our new soda launch. In exchange for their usual fees and free product, they'd each promote our different soda flavors, with the last leg of the campaign focusing entirely on CitraCrush."

I nod slowly, trying to give the impression I understand this completely. It figures, I can run complex array functions in Excel in my sleep, but this sounds like a foreign language.

There's a heavy pause and I realize she's now waiting for me to say something, only I still have no idea where to begin. My pulse thrums in my neck, heart rate climbing from the anxiety of it all. I tap my pen against my still-blank legal pad, willing words, any words, to come to my lips.

Cate clears her throat, a look akin to concern passing over her face, and I try not to groan. How did she end up with the upper hand in this?

"When we left things on Wednesday, it sounded like the campaign would be over our budget. Maybe it would be good to start with what our budget cap is and go from there?"

I practically sigh with relief, my head bobs growing more erratic. A task, something I can do. I swivel a few inches to the left and pull up the budget sheets on my computer screen. And then the smile that had been spreading across my lips stops dead in its tracks.

Right. Her budget is already stretched further than it should be, considering we missed our targets last quarter.

Frowning at the screen, I pull up a copy of her slide deck to double check the estimate she'd provided, thinking maybe I'd misremembered.

I swivel back to Cate, lips turned down. "It looks like you projected a budget of one hundred thousand for the entire campaign." She nods shallowly and I continue, "Unfortunately, with our other allocated costs, we've only got about twenty-five thousand left over."

Her eyes bulge out of her head, which was the exact reaction I expected. Or maybe I'd pictured her slamming her laptop shut and hurling it across the tiny room at me, the defined muscles in her arms rippling.

Not that I've noticed them before. Her arms. And certainly not her legs, currently on full display in a pair of pleated, tailored shorts.

She seems to be holding herself back, trying to keep her volume at a reasonable level when she asks, "That's all we can spare?"

I glance back at my monitor, willing the numbers to show me something different and knowing they won't. Can't. Pressing my lips into a thin line that I hope looks apologetic and not snobbish, I shake my head.

She blows out a breath and leans back in her seat, shifting her legs so they're crossed at the ankle now. I force my gaze to her face and swallow, trying to think of some sort of alternative. For reasons I don't fully understand, it's clear this is important to her.

"You mentioned this relies on us partnering with multiple influencers," I say slowly, and she slides her gaze back to mine. "We clearly don't have the money to work with all of them, but what if we cut down to a few?"

"We'd barely be able to afford one with that." She laughs without humor.

I twist my mouth to one side. That doesn't make any sense. She has ten people listed on that slide deck, I just checked.

When I share that with her, she gusts out the heaviest sigh I've ever heard, like she can't even believe she needs to explain this. She leans forward to type something on her computer, then turns the screen around to face me. On it is a social media profile for a woman named Lauren Roth. I recall the name from the deck, but the relevance here is lost on me otherwise. Cocking my head at Cate, I will her to go on.

"Yes, there were ten influencers total. But this is the most important—and most expensive—one. The first nine partners combined accounted for about seventy-five percent of the cost. Lauren was the rest."

"And she'd be the one releasing the new flavor?"

Cate nods and I roll my bottom lip between my teeth.

"I admit, I don't understand much about"—I wave a hand vaguely at the profile in front of me—"but wouldn't it make the most sense to forget Lauren and try to partner with as many of the others as we can with our budget?"

Cate blinks rapidly, her chin jutting out. "I'm guessing you didn't read the additional resources I had linked to in my slide deck?"

I sputter a bit but can't form words. In short: No, no I did not.

An unreadable look passes over her face. "Based on my research, and given this is a new product launch, I think we'd get more brand exposure and engagement from potential buyers by working with her specifically."

Unable to stop myself, I shoot back, "What are these people even going to post? It seems incredulous for them to charge this much." I cross my arms over my chest and level my chin at her. "Can't we do this ourselves?"

Cate blinks slowly at me, like I suggested she make a peanut butter and toothpaste sandwich. The professional tone she's tried to maintain this entire time falters when she says, "Sure, let me spend countless hours cultivating a digital lifestyle brand and millions of followers. Totally reasonable to do in less than two months."

I roll my head from one side to the other, some of my bravado blowing out. "Point taken. But still, wouldn't doing this ourselves be the better long-term investment? Sure it'll be hard, but we'd get all the return." It's my turn to blink slowly at Cate, like I've solved world hunger and she's too pigheaded to see it.

"In case you hadn't noticed," she says, crossing her arms under her chest in a way that further opens up the scoop neck of her shirt. My eyes track the movement and, before I can look away, a pulsing heat spreads under the collar of my shirt. "Our social media team is basically me, Mindy, and an intern right now. Something like this requires creativity, resources, equipment. Most importantly, it takes time. Time we don't have."

For the second time in this meeting, the unfamiliar desire to win her over becomes an unbearable nagging sensation at the back of my skull. "So I'll help you."

CHAPTER 7

Cate

I'M NOT SURE WHICH one of us is more surprised to hear those words come out of his mouth, me or Paul. Judging by the way his eyebrows climb his forehead, it may be him.

If I had attempted to make any predictions about the outcome of this meeting, this would have been at the bottom of the list. Right behind *a gigantic sinkhole opens up in the middle of the office and swallows us whole* and *the planet is overtaken by aliens.*

"You," I say after opening and closing my mouth noiselessly a few times. "You're going to help?" My tone is flat, skeptical. I can't help it. One offer isn't going to change two years of animosity.

Paul seems frozen again. I've come to recognize it as his signature look. New this time: there's a red flush creeping out of the crisp white collar of his shirt. My mind drifts to this morning, when I saw him at the gym. It was the first time I'd seen him wear anything else. A V-neck T-shirt, no less! I'd lingered a little too long on a tuft of blond hair on his chest, visible where the fabric dipped down, and I'd wanted to punch myself.

Right as I'm about to fake a cough into my hand to thaw him, he says, "Sure, why not?"

Though there are a million reasons that come to mind, not a single one of them is appropriate to say to a colleague. I settle for slack-jawed silence.

Paul doubles down, leaning forward so his elbows are braced against the desk. His sleeves strain against his forearms, cuffed tightly around his wrists, hinting at sinewy muscle beneath. "I have a little bit of video experience. We could probably use our phones for most of it and dip into the software budget for what we don't have." I've never seen him look this excited before, a light dancing behind his eyes that wasn't even there when he gave me the smackdown on Monday. As a matter of fact, he'd looked a little defeated. Like the report he was presenting had insulted him on a personal level. Odd.

His bright idea is for us to film our own videos leading up to the product launch and post them on the brand social media accounts. We can still do it like I'd planned, showing off all our existing sodas before revealing the newest flavor, he tells me. Then we can spring for Lauren Roth at the end using what's left of my budget.

It's official, he's totally lost it. I always thought I'd feel more gratification when this moment arrived. I imagined him having some sort of nervous breakdown, one where he thinks he's being attacked by his own spreadsheets, so this is a bit disappointing. Still, right now all I feel is concern. And a little scared. For him, but also for me and my legacy here at VitaPop. My shot at an Edie Award, dashed.

"Come on, Cate! This could work. And even if it isn't the original plan, you still get Lauren Roth." He's smiling now, not quite a grin, but still the biggest sweep and dip of his lips I've ever witnessed. It's hard not to absorb some of it, the first ray of sunlight after an especially cold winter.

I'm still not ready to stop looking for excuses though. Ten minutes ago this guy didn't even know who Lauren Roth was, and now he's saying her name with the triumph of someone who finally hugged their celebrity crush. "And you have no problem being in the videos?"

For the first time since he hatched this hair-brained scheme, indecision passes over Paul's face. I simply arch my eyebrows. It's clear he pictured himself behind-the-scenes in this equation, but a social media collaborator who can't be on camera is useless to me. No one wants to watch the same exact person do the same things over and over with no variety. I think I've finally caught him. It's strangely disappointing.

After a few beats, he nods. "Yeah, fine, that's no problem." His mouth is still twisted in thought. "We have to come up with an idea though, like you said."

Wow, Paul Andrews actually paid attention to me. Alert the media.

"We can't simply review our own products like the content creators would have. It'll seem disingenuous. No one wants to watch a brand pat itself on the back," I argue before he can suggest it.

Surprisingly, he nods again. "No, of course not. We need something unique. Something that feels like it *should* be coming from us."

We both look off into the middle distance, the room silent but for the gears whirring in our heads. After a few oddly comfortable minutes, I snap my fingers. "Recipes!"

Paul tilts his head in my direction. "Recipes?"

"Yeah, but not your run-of-the-mill recipes. We find unique ingredients to mix with the different VitaPop sodas. Then make, taste, and rate them on camera."

"Okay," he says slowly, so it comes out like *ooookaaaaay*.

"It wouldn't have to be only sodas either! We could incorporate the mix-in powders and the juices we sell too." I can see it in my head. Cocktails, mocktails, unique twists on all our core flavors.

He smiles, a painfully slow curve of his mouth, and if I thought his earlier one had been something to bask in, this one threatens to drown me. Apparently Paul Andrews has dimples, and I have the strange urge to swim in them.

Cocking his head to one side, he raps his knuckles against his faux marble desk. "Let's go tell Darius the plan." The plan. Something in the way he says it makes my toes curl, my pulse thrum in my veins.

For the third time today, this man has surprised me.

CHAPTER 8

Cate

PAUL MIGHT BE REGRETTING all of the life decisions he's made in the past twenty-four hours. They've landed him—both of us—back at the VitaPop office on a Saturday afternoon. The ingredients for our first video are sprawled before us on the wide island in the company's test kitchen.

The kitchen itself is a small room on the other side of our break area, equipped with a few stainless steel appliances—a commercial refrigerator, an oven and stove combo, and a large basin sink—and a laminate-topped island that takes up almost every free inch of space left over. When the company first started, it's where they used to test new product ideas. Now, VitaPop has a separate facility a few miles from the corporate office with a lot more space.

For us, the tiny space is perfect. It's painted in neutral colors that won't look garish on camera and has a good bit of natural light coming in through three large panel windows lining one wall.

The last few minutes, Paul has been picking up each ingredient on the island and reading the nutrition labels, the curl in his upper lip growing. I duck my head, pretending to adjust our tabletop tripod, to hide my amusement.

Darius took little convincing yesterday when we'd popped by his office to pitch our new and *yet-to-be-decided-if-it's-improved* idea. He heard "budget-friendly" and "Lauren Roth" in the same breath, and that was enough.

For him, the social media campaign is probably the cherry on top of all the work he's done the past year with the commercial planning teams. Whether Paul and I succeed or fail, Darius has a sweet partnership with some of the most well-known health grocery chains in the country, plus a traditional advertising buy I helped negotiate, to fall back on.

And he's getting Lauren Roth. Make that two cherries on top.

This is so much bigger than that for me. Sure, I helped with his marketing plan, but this campaign is *mine*. Something to call my own. My claim to Edie Award fame.

Or, at least it was.

I glance at Paul again when I'm sure I've got the angle right on the tripod. He has his palms braced against the counter, dead center in the frame like he's supposed to be there. He doesn't look half bad there either.

I'd expected him to show up in yet another pair of khaki slacks and his signature white button-down. He'd shown me up though, dressed plainly—in a good way, for once—in a pair of dark blue jeans that hug his thighs and loosen near his ankles and a navy sweater. The color of it almost matches his eyes. Paul's version of weekend casual, I guess.

"This looks disgusting," he says, snapping my focus. The sound echoes in the eerie quiet, the entire campus deserted except for the lone janitor responsible for keeping the place tidy. Every once in a while I hear him pass by the entrance to the kitchen with his orbital floor scrubber, leaving a wet slice of concrete floor in his wake.

I suppress a snort and come around the island to stand beside Paul. He doesn't register my presence, still focused on the spread before him.

"We'll find out soon enough," I sing, and now he shoots me a horrified look.

"You mean you've never tried this before?"

"Nope," I say, popping the P at the end. "But it's trending right now, and Mindy said it's not half-bad."

"Oh, well if Mindy says it." He stabs a rough hand through his hair in exasperation. The ends of it are still slightly damp, like he showered right before meeting me here.

It makes me feel a little self-conscious. I'd had enough time after my rugby game to change into a brown skort, burgundy turtleneck, and my favorite brown heeled boots, but I hadn't had enough time to shower. Instead, I doused myself in deodorant, body spray, and dry shampoo, hoping it would give the illusion of one.

Paul doesn't seem to notice, instead continuing on his diatribe. "It even sounds disgusting: dirty soda. Who wants to drink something with dirty right there in the name? It's like a warning."

This time I can't restrain my scoff, but I do try to mask it by pulling the cute glassware I found for a steal at the local dollar store and a bowl of large ice cubes closer to us. "Relax, it's just a name." *And if you hate it, it'll only make your reaction even funnier to watch.*

It had been Paul's idea to start with something a little more off the wall than my original suggestion: a crisp cranberry and apple cocktail, crafted with our antioxidant rich CranCraze juice and our prebiotic apple soda—and perfect for the transition to fall we're starting to see here in the Pacific Northwest.

I'd surprised both of us by conceding. Which is why I'm now delighting in the fact that I get to force feed him a drink made of VitaPop's diet cola soda and a homemade pumpkin cold foam topped with cinnamon.

Honestly, it doesn't sound bad to me, but something about the combination of bubbles and milk product skeeves Paul out. He's told me as much about a dozen times. And even if he hadn't, I've caught him shivering and making a *blech* face at least four other times when he thought I wasn't looking. Maybe Mindy was right and this whole partnership thing wouldn't be so bad after all.

"Are you only filming it vertically?"

Or maybe she was wrong. "Yes," I say curtly. *Duh.* Out of the corner of my eye, Paul is fiddling with the frother we'll use to make the cold foam.

"I was doing some research last night, about social media strategy." The look I send his way makes him stop short. He wets his lips and blood thunders in my ears. "I thought maybe we could cross-post these to YouTube."

"We don't use YouTube." *Didn't notice that in all your "research," did you?*

Paul leans his hip against the counter. Well, with his height, it's more like he's leaning his side butt against it. And now I'm thinking about Paul Andrews's butt and that simply must stop, so I meet his gaze and try to keep an open mind. We've made it this far. If there's a chance I can salvage a decent campaign out of this, I have to embrace it.

"I know, but I thought maybe we could give it a shot with this series. See how it goes."

I fold my arms under my chest and this time I'm sure I see him glance down and then quickly back up. *Interesting.* Out loud, I say, "Fine, but you're on YouTube duty. I don't have as much experience with that platform and my video editing skills aren't as strong as Mindy's." I have no issues creating simple videos on my phone for social media, but when we need to produce something high quality, I pull her in. She's a wizard with all the major video-editing tools: After Effects, Premiere Pro, Final Cut Pro, you name it.

Paul looks taken aback for a fleeting moment and I furrow my brows, wondering why. Then I realize, it's probably the first time I've admitted to a fault in my skills at work. And in front of this man, my sworn enemy, no less. Standing up a little straighter, I drop my arms to brush the front of my skort and slide my attention to something else. Anything else.

Eagerly, like he's afraid I might change my mind, Paul pulls his phone and a tripod like mine from his backpack. "Of course, I'll handle it, no problem," he assures me while setting them up on the counter, his phone tilted horizontally for a wider angle.

I watch him fuss with it for a few seconds, studying the way his nimble fingers swipe against the phone screen and carefully tweak the legs of the tripod until it's just so. He's precise and seems more comfortable than I would have expected.

Maybe his fun Friday-night research taught him how to shoot video too. Even my inner monologue wants to mock this guy.

CHAPTER 9

Paul

OUR FIRST TIME FILMING together went about as wrong as it possibly could have.

To start, the recipe was built for disaster, as I told Cate many, many times. Who mixes dairy products and soda? It's barbaric.

On top of that, Cate purposely asked me to froth the cream to create the pumpkin cold foam. It wasn't like I could openly admit to never having used a frother before, though it was the first time I'd ever laid eyes on one. I didn't realize it had multiple speed settings until it was too late and I'd already sent cream flying all over the faux marble countertop.

And one of my favorite sweaters. I had to wear an apron we found buried in the test kitchen's pantry for the rest of the shoot.

Things improved with my second attempt, and despite knowing what it was made out of, the drink looked decent enough by the end. Tasted awful though, as expected. Cate had the audacity to say she thought it was good. *Pretty okay* had been her exact words, which

I guess didn't classify as a rave review. She probably only said it to disagree with me.

For everything that went wrong though, the footage was perfect. After we'd cleaned up our mess, Cate plopped down on one of the uncomfortable-looking bar stools bordering one side of the island and immediately started working on her phone. I'd kept a few feet away, arms hanging awkwardly by my sides, knowing I'd need an actual laptop to cut together a video high-quality enough for YouTube.

Seconds later, she waved me over to show me her first clip: me, front and center with the frother, spraying cream all over the place. She'd added some sort of effect that made it flash and replay dozens of times across the screen at different speeds and angles. I pursed my lips, shooting her my best *are you kidding me?* look, but she'd only beamed back, long blonde hair swishing against her back as she craned her exposed neck to meet my gaze.

As perturbed as I was, it took everything in me not to grin back, the expression on her face infectious. Finally, I'd earned one of those elusive smiles. I may have had to make an utter fool of myself to get one, but I've been in worse situations.

My overwhelming desire to do it again, to earn that look from her, made my stomach drop.

As hilarious as Cate thought it was, we agreed we couldn't post that, at least not right now—the recipe had to come first, to set the tone for the series, she explained matter-of-factly—so I set off for home and the Premiere Pro subscription I still paid for on my personal computer. I could never bring myself to cancel it after high school, the last time I'd used it to edit any videos.

I spent the better part of my Saturday evening working, pausing only to order Thai from a local place that delivers for a premium. It was easy, even after a years-long hiatus, to pick it back up. That familiar rush of adrenaline when you nail a sequence—adjusting the levels, adding transitions, smoothing out the lighting until it's perfectly balanced. I'd missed it. Things I'd been so good at before. Things I thought I'd forgotten.

Things I thought I'd never do again.

Now that it's time to show it to Cate, though, my palms are slick with perspiration. My chest is tight, breath coming heavy. I'm *nervous*.

It's Tuesday and we're back in my office for our new weekly planning meeting. Yes, we went from never speaking to having a re-curring time blocked on our calendars to work together. Somebody run outside to check for flying pigs.

She's perched in the same chair she had claimed last Friday when we first started on this journey, wearing a small satisfied smile. We just watched the vertical video she'd cut together in a little under a half hour on her phone. It's short, snappy, funny. Good. I admitted as much to her, hence the smile.

My video is different. Longer, but I wouldn't call it more serious. I left her a little surprise at the end, so eager to earn that look of approval again. Too eager. A puppy who successfully performed its first trick. It's not a welcome thought, only adding to my nausea.

When Cate makes a choking sound while watching it, halfway between a barking laugh and what could best be described as a dog sneezing, I know I've succeeded. She presses pause on the video seconds before the end and lifts her chin to face me, eyes bright and lips curved. "You added a blooper reel." It's not quite a question, the way she says it, but I get the sense it demands an answer.

I dip my head in a small nod. "You were right, those clips were funny." We can still post them separately as shorts to YouTube, but I thought this was a fun little Easter egg for people tuning into our first video.

She pins me across my desk with a smug look and asks, "Can I get that in writing?" Not following the non sequitur, I arch one eyebrow, the other dipping low over my eye.

"You admitting I was right." She pauses to reach for her phone. "Actually, why don't you say it again for the camera?"

I roll my eyes, though it bears no weight, and come around the desk so we can watch the last few seconds of the video together. Too late, I realize how close my chest needs to get to her shoulder to press play on her computer. How my nose nearly skims her neck. She smells like flowers, like she always does, but also something else. A scent I can't place, but one that takes me back to hiking the Redwoods at sixteen, fresh-faced and overconfident. As soon as my index finger taps her keyboard, I pull away.

Fortunately, Cate doesn't seem to notice, drawn to the end of the blooper reel. The last clip is of the two of us tasting the drink, my sour pucker and bunched shoulders next to her upside-down smile and casual shrug. At the same time she says, "Not bad," I say, "That's terrible," and then we both burst into laughter. I had to watch it at least a hundred times when making this video, but it still makes me squirm to see it again. Hers is so boisterous, demanding attention, and mine is more reserved, almost contemplative. The opposites should look strange together. Wrong, like they don't belong in the same room. Instead, it's probably the best clip we got.

"You edited this?" Cate asks, dragging me back to the present. Taking my seat across from her again, I try not to take offense at the surprise in her tone. She doesn't know I used to stay up way too late in high school, making videos. Or why I stopped.

I respond with a dip of my chin so she can't read my face.

"It's good," she says slowly, unsure. "You've done this before." Another not-question-question.

Even though I knew to expect this, I stiffen in my chair. Why does she have to be so damn perceptive?

The entire time I'd been editing, reacquainting myself with the software, I'd also been at war with myself. *Cate's sharp*, I told myself, *she'll have questions*. How'd I learn this software? Did I make videos regularly? Could she see them? I'd played it all out in my head and confirmed I'm not ready to have this conversation. Not with Cate, not with anyone.

But by then, it was too late to turn back. This was my idea. She'd put me in charge of it. I had to follow through.

Besides, if she's curious enough and a little bit patient, she could figure it out on her own. Find the videos my friends and I posted on YouTube back then, when I was still learning. Then again, I'm pretty sure patience is not Cate's strong suit. In fact, I'm betting on it.

The half-truth I prepared slips out easier than I thought it would. "Took a few classes in high school and college. The tool is basic enough. It was easy to pick most of it back up. I Googled the rest."

She searches my face, and it's hard not to wither beneath her penetrating stare. Whatever she's looking for, she either finds it or decides she doesn't care. With a small nod, she pivots to ask, "You ready?" and I loosen my stance a fraction of an inch.

We're ceremonious without meaning to be, both of us pushing the publish buttons at the same time. Two videos that should, in theory, be the same, and yet they could not be more different. Like their creators.

For seconds, I don't think either of us takes a breath. And then... nothing happens. Not that we expected it to, deep down.

"It'll probably take some time," she says, letting her phone screen go dark.

"Right," I reply, because I'm not sure what else to say. Only that I want to keep talking, which is odd. That I'm not ready for her to walk away and take the scent of peonies and rain with her.

I cough into a fist, then blurt out the first thing I can think of. "Have you decided when you plan to post the other video?" The one of me.

One corner of her mouth drags up. "Itching for fame already?" she teases and I pinch my mouth into a thin line. "I'm not sure yet. I'd like to give this one a chance to circulate first, and maybe add a few more like it so viewers can tell it's a series."

Cate glances down at her phone where a few views have slowly trickled in. No engagement yet, though. "You know what? Let's hope by this time tomorrow, we're *both* famous."

I know it's a joke, that I should chuckle, but instead I frown. After all our time working on this, I can't believe I hadn't thought of it before now. If this goes well, if we succeed, there's no way someone from my family won't see it—see me—and start to ask questions. No way it won't get back to my father. Probably the only person in the world who was happy to see me put my video editing days behind me.

My stomach clenches, but there's also a small fire burning in my chest, one that screams *let him see it*.

"When are you free again this week?" Cate asks, and I blink at her. "So we can film the next one. I want to try the cocktail idea out." *Ah.*

I set the pen I've been fiddling with for the past few minutes down and check the calendar on my laptop. Like I don't already know what's on it. It's not that I don't have meetings, I do, but they're recurring and typically scheduled well in advance. Unless it's an emergency or a problem (or both, in most cases), I don't get surprises.

"Did you still want to go to the orchard for part of that one?"

She'd slipped the idea in at the tail end of filming on Saturday, when we were already out the door and halfway across the parking lot from one another. I imagine it was a tactic, one meant to catch me off guard, and it worked. I'd sputtered instead of protesting and by the time I'd had a moment to think about it she was already diving into the driver's side of her Nissan and shouting, "Cool, I'll send you the details, thanks!"

Now she straightens in her chair, angling her chin at me in a way that dares me to try to talk her out of it. "Yeah, we can pick a few apples, get some B-roll, then come back here for the rest."

I blow a long exhale through my nose to buy some time. Something about going off-campus with Cate feels like I've been casually asked to climb Mount Everest. I've never met with coworkers outside of the office before, unless it was a *not-mandatory-but-really-mandatory* team building event. In fact, I can't remember the last time I went out with friends, period. Unless you count my cousin who moved here to Seattle about a year ago and occasionally drags me out for drinks or dinner.

A few of my buddies from UW still live in the area, but maintaining those friendships as an adult, when there's work and hobbies and romantic relationships (theirs, not mine) all pulling you away from one another? It's hard. And I haven't tried much, either.

Those people only know part of who I am, the part that was born at eighteen.

But the orchard is probably a good idea. Not only will it give us B-roll for this one video, we might be able to milk a few more out of it.

"Are you available tomorrow after work? Shady Tree opens at four," I say after pulling up their website. I'd never heard of the little farm about a thirty-minute drive from our office before Cate suggested it.

She smiles, satisfied, and stands. "Great, it's a—" She hesitates in front of the door, the color draining from her face at the same moment mine does. Grabbing hastily for the metal handle of the glass door to my office, she tosses back over her shoulder, "See you then," instead and plows through it.

CHAPTER 10

Cate

A LITTLE GIRL, PROBABLY no older than six, plummets down a dark green slide in the center of a well-kept playground. One of those new plastic deals, the kind that burns up in the peak summer sun and fries the back of your legs like bacon in a pan when you slide down it. It's built into the side of a jungle gym designed to look like a castle, complete with a fake drawbridge that splits it down the middle.

Today is a comfortable sixty-four degrees, perfect for sliding. The peal of laughter she sends up after reaching the bottom makes my lips quirk. The second the slide spits her out, she scrabbles back to the ladder for another go. It will be impossible to drag her away from it when it's time to leave, like it was for me at that age. The raging temper tantrums I would throw when my parents tried to pry me away from the jungle gym could go in parenting textbooks: *How to Handle Your Impossible Toddler.*

It got to the point where my parents dreaded every trip to the playground at the end of our street with the giant wooden castle standing proudly at its center, until the trips stopped altogether. By the time my younger sister was old enough to go, I was no longer interested in joining them.

The jungle gyms may not be wooden anymore—these new plastic ones last a lot longer so the buyer gets their money's worth—but some things never change.

Frowning, I turn away from the slide and the little girl only to run smack dab into Paul Andrews on his trek from the parking lot. My stomach flips at the sight of him in faded charcoal jeans and a thin gray crew neck sweater that stretches across his chest until it looks threadbare. I'm only too happy to be dragged from my thoughts, but still try to restrain my smile. After all, this is Paul. I can't seem too cheerful to see him.

"Am I late?" he asks, quirking an eyebrow and glancing meaningfully between me and the playground.

"Nope, I'm early." We briefly, *briefly* discussed carpooling here, but we live in completely opposite directions. On the surface, driving separately was practical. Going deeper, it was wise.

"Wanted to get a few rounds in before we start?"

I furrow my brow and study his face. Only then do I notice the small uptick in one corner of his mouth and the way his chin tips toward the playground. My mouth drops open. *Did Paul Andrews crack a joke?*

I must've accidentally said that out loud, because the curve on his lips stretches wider. "I've been known to do so on occasion. About every five years or so." Something about the deadpan way he says it only makes it funnier. And more shocking. I think my eyes might bug out of my head.

Pursing my lips to hold back laughter, I fall into step beside him and we make our way to the little red shed at the center of the property. After securing a small bushel basket for apples, we follow the attendant's directions down the orchard's main lane in a comfortable silence until we reach the first grove of Ambrosia apple trees.

When the word "comfortable" decided to associate itself with Paul and me, I do not know. Maybe it was when I helped clean some of the pumpkin cold foam out of his hair after he'd sprayed it all over the place. Or maybe it was our shared commiseration over the way our first recipe video flopped. Between TikTok and YouTube, we barely scraped together 400 views. The algorithms hated us. The day we'd finally given up on it going any higher, he'd sent me a gif of Patrick Star crying on Slack and it weirdly cheered me up.

Either way, I'm beginning to find it's not entirely unpleasant, spending time with him. I can't even remember the last time I made a snide comment about him and meant it.

It's still early enough in the season that the apples have just begun to ripen and the trees are still chock full of the red-and-yellow fruit. Starting this weekend, crowds of families, couples, and friends will flock here to deplete their bounty. For today, it's all ours.

The slowly sinking sun casts a bronze-ish glow through the grove, its light dappling through the branches and leaves to warm the ground below. Now that we're here, the whole place to ourselves, my palms start to sweat. I hadn't thought about how intimate this would be.

Like a date.

I study the trees to avoid looking at Paul.

He, on the other hand, seems to have no such concerns. "I'll grab some B-roll of the trees if you want to start picking apples." There's no waver to his voice, no tremble in his hands as he hooks his phone into a small stabilizer and heads to where the trees are thickest, the complete opposite direction of where I'm standing.

Okay, so maybe not date-like at all. That's totally fine. Absolutely fine. Good even. So why do I feel so on edge? My stomach twists the same way it does on the rugby pitch right before the opposing team makes a play for the ball. Defensive.

I choose to ignore it, hike up the bushel basket in my hands, and get to work. By the time Paul finds me again, my basket is half full.

"Ready to move on to the Honeycrisp?"

I startle at the sound of his voice and drop an apple. It teeters to the ground, slowly rolling top over bottom until it comes to rest at Paul's feet. Juice leaks out of it from a large bite in its side and I drop my eyes in embarrassment.

He looks pointedly from the apple to me and his answering smirk twists my insides in a knot. The feeling is unfamiliar, somewhere between murderous and craving. I swallow it down, hoping it disappears altogether, and march toward him with my head high.

"They're best when they're fresh," I toss over my shoulder, prancing right past him in the direction of the next grove, expecting him to follow.

Fortunately, or unfortunately depending on that strange knot in my stomach, he does. "Wasn't going to say a thing." His voice is low, like a hum, and it strums against my skin like fingers dancing across guitar strings. *Dammit, Cate. Get it together. This is your mortal enemy.*

My strides are unnecessarily long, booted feet slipping in the dewy grass of the lane until a sign bearing "Honeycrisp" in untidy cursive comes into view. I'm half-panting from the effort by the time I reach it. Meanwhile, the beanpole and his monstrously long legs have no trouble keeping up, much to my dismay.

"It's my first time," he says when we reach the tree line, so quiet I almost miss it.

My head swings on my shoulders, eyes narrowing. "First time?"

He has the good sense to look sheepish, shoving his hands into his pockets. "At an orchard."

"You're lying," I accuse before I can stop myself, then immediately clamp my big mouth shut. I'm not sure why it's the first thing I think of, but even *I've* gone apple-picking with my family before. There's no way perfect Paul with his perfect life hasn't.

He shrugs, looks around. "I mean, I went pumpkin-picking a few times as a kid. But never apples."

It's an olive branch, I realize. Rather than reveling in my embarrassment, I think he's trying to make me feel better. Or at least change the subject. It's like this project opened a portal to another world where Paul and I are friends. That's the only reasonable explanation.

I exhale through my nose and nod, one corner of my lips lifting. "In that case, you need the full experience." Yep, I've officially left the planet.

Ignoring the confusion that flits across his face, I trudge straight into the center of the Honeycrisp trees, feeling my way along the trunks and boughs, eyes squinting at the fruit weighing them down.

Seconds later, Paul's right on my tail. "What are you doing?"

"What's it look like I'm doing?"

"I'm not sure. It looks like you might be trying to find the door to a hidden realm," he remarks drily, chin pointed at my probing hands.

I can't hold back my answering snort. "You've seen too many movies."

"Actually I've read the books," he says, and without spelling it out somehow I know he's referencing *The Lion, the Witch and the Wardrobe*. "The books are always better."

I choose to ignore the comment, stopping short to pull back from the apple tree and grin up at the tallest branch. He doesn't have enough time to compensate and his chest collides with my back. Normally, I'd call him on it, maybe fake an injury, but I'm feeling charitable today. I keep my mouth zipped tight while he staggers a couple steps away. It's yet another sign that my armor is weakening and needs replaced.

Hands on my hips, I nod at an apple on the highest bough. It's perfect. A little asymmetrical on top, but very round. The perfect amount of greenish-yellow color streaking through the fire-engine red skin. It shines, but not from a chemical wash. "There," I say, reverently.

"Congratulations, you found an apple. In an apple tree. In an orchard."

The urge to tackle Paul Andrews rears up again, and it should feel like a homecoming. Instead it fills my head with images that don't belong there and makes my neck feel hot and prickly.

Pushing them away, I brace the length of my body against the tree trunk, right arm reaching. "Everyone knows the first thing you do at an apple orchard is find the best apple and eat it, right off the branch. Apples always taste better when they're fresh and they don't have that weird coating they get at the grocery store to make them last longer," I explain through my straining. It's no use. Even on my tip-toes, with my arm stretched as far out of the socket as it will go, I'm about a foot shy.

I pull back and root my hands against my hips, leveling a determined glare at the apple. I don't have time to battle a new nemesis. While I cock my head, considering, Paul moves past me and takes my place.

He braces his left hand against the trunk at about chest level, the veins in his forearms dancing under his rolled-up sleeves. The hem of his sweater slides a few inches up his back, revealing a deep ripple of muscle just above the waistband of his jeans. My mouth waters against my will and I tear my eyes away, focusing on the apple instead. One of the comments from our first video together comes to mind: "Why he kinda...?"

A flash of annoyance flames to life in my chest and I have to press a hand to it to stifle the sensation. Why should I care if a few weirdos on the Internet decided to thirst over him? It's a free country.

The pain dulls then, replaced by a small sense of satisfaction when even he, Mr. Beanpole himself, can't reach the apple. I smirk at him when he spins around, hoping the flush I still feel in my face from watching him isn't visible on the outside.

If it is, he doesn't say anything, instead throwing his hands out to the sides so he looks like the shrugging emoji. "Let's find a different one." How strange it is, that casual use of "us" and the way it makes my heart race.

Focus, Cate! Right, I'm not giving up that easily. I don't give up, period.

Stepping to his side, I point at his legs. "Here, bend your knee and give me a boost."

He blinks at me like I grew five heads, and a groan rumbles in the back of my throat. I'm standing in front of an accountant and still I'm the smartest person in the orchard.

"If you make a little step out of your thigh, I can stand on it and brace myself against the tree. It'll give me an extra foot or so," I explain, trying to pantomime what I mean with my body.

He frowns and looks down at himself. "But these are my favorite jeans."

My jaw unhinges like a snake's, eyelids drooping in disbelief. "Do you want a fresh apple or not?"

"It seems more like you want a fresh apple," he grumbles so I barely hear him and yes, any weird feelings of desire are totally snuffed out now. The murderous rage is back, an old friend.

Paul must see it in my expression because he releases a deep sigh through his mouth. "Fine," he mutters, moving closer to the tree then dropping into a modified lunge.

A satisfied smile sweeps across my lips and I stomp right up to him. I place my left foot on his thigh as indelicately as possible and push off with my right until I'm springing into the air faster than I mean to. I have to smack my hands against the thin tree trunk to brace myself, my weight shifting unevenly forward and then back.

A strong hand meets the small of my back, steadying me. It's surprisingly warm through the thin fabric of my sweater. I can feel the press of each individual fingertip as if there was nothing there at all. The resolve I felt moments ago wavers, and I bite my bottom lip.

When I first hatched this plan, I thought I'd be more in the tree, but from this position I ended up more on top of Paul. My hip is a fraction of an inch from his chest. His hand is about the same distance from the top of my ass. I try to keep my attention focused on the branches above my head, on anything else, but I'm frozen. I know the way the small heels of my boots are digging into his leg has to be uncomfortable, but Paul doesn't seem fazed at all.

Great, so on top of being completely infuriating, he's also a superhero.

The tops of his fingers dig into my back, a small push of encouragement, and my muscles unseize. This is fine. He doesn't think it's weird. Don't make it weird.

I stretch my body skyward, reaching my right arm as high as it will go, but this time my fingers finally close around the bottom edge of the once-forbidden fruit. *Got it!* I give it a gentle pull to release the stem from the branch, but it doesn't budge. Even with the extra boost, I still don't have quite enough leverage.

At this point, I'm in too deep. Failure is not an option. My ass is literally in Paul Andrews's face. I cannot come back down empty-handed. With my jaw set, I grip the apple harder and tug firmly. Only this time, it's too firmly. When the apple comes loose, the force sends my wrist arcing back behind my head, and my balance goes right along with it.

Then I'm falling, the grassy earth rising to meet me like a cresting wave. It's all I can do to twist my body toward it, trying to put my hands between myself and the ground. With my eyes shut tight for impact, I expect to feel nothing but cold, hard dampness against my front. Instead, I hit something warm and firm but also soft and yielding at the same time.

Oh god. Blinking open my eyes slowly, I find Paul beneath me, our faces level, my boobs crushed against his hard chest in a way that makes me tingle and shiver and writhe all at the same time. He must've sensed my impending fall and tried to catch me. *Damn you, superhero Paul.*

For long seconds, we simply stare at each other, the tips of our noses a hair's breadth from touching. When sensation returns to my body, I realize I'm gripping his shoulders and that his big hands are cradling my waist. I realize that our breaths are in sync, chests moving together like one body. I realize my right knee is pressed between his thighs and then all my concentration centers in that one spot until I can't think about anything else.

Until I notice the way Paul's gaze drifts between my eyes and my lips in a cyclical pattern. Then all I can think about is his mouth, so close to mine. What it might feel like. Are his lips hard, like the rest of his body? Or are they soft, inviting, well-cared for with routine applications of Chapstick and maybe a lip mask once a week?

Knowing him, it's probably the latter. I subconsciously wet my lips with the tip of my tongue and I swear I hear Paul sigh from somewhere deep in his throat and *god*, that sound! That sound makes me shudder, makes me arch my back, makes my fingers dig into his round shoulders until—

Something plunks against the ground right beside Paul's head and startles us both. It happens again, this time the culprit thwacking me in the back of the knee. Within seconds, a barrage of Honeycrisp apples falls down around us, my aggressive tugging in the tree obviously knocking some of the ripest ones loose.

One drops and hits Paul in the side of the head, and my mouth springs open as wide as my eyes. Then I'm biting back a riotous fit of giggles, trying in vain to stifle the sound. He lifts a hand from my waist to rub the sore spot, wincing at his own touch, and it releases the floodgates fully until I'm arched backward, cackling in the most unattractive way possible.

And then he's laughing too. The sound starts as a low rumble in his chest that vibrates throughout my body, then progresses until he's howling as loud as I am.

He'll never forget his first time visiting an apple orchard, and now neither will I.

CHAPTER 11

Paul

MY ARMS SHAKE UNDER the weight of the dumbbells in my hands, a drop of sweat beading over my eyebrow and straight into my right eye. I blink rapidly to clear my vision, my reflection in the wall of mirrors before me blurring as I strain against the last curl in my set.

The sun is starting to shift the world outside the gym's floor-to-ceiling windows from slate to a brighter, smoky gray. Early enough to, hopefully, prevent any possible interruptions this time. I'd thought about coming this afternoon, then remembered I'm meeting Cate to shoot another video and struck that out. Our second video, the apple-flavored cocktail Cate cooked up, bombed nearly as bad as our first. It's time to change up our strategy.

Then I'd debated skipping the gym altogether, but that's the type of thinking that leads to broken habits and then bad ones. At least that's what my dad says. There was a time in my life where I would've done exactly that, solely because it went against what he wanted for me. Expected of me. It seems that part of me died ten years ago on that mountain too. I've fallen in line.

I carefully place the weights back in their rack right as my phone vibrates in my pocket, interrupting the pounding guitar and drum beats playing through my headphones. My stomach bottoms out. There's only two people in this world whose phone calls can get through my Do Not Disturb setting. A glance down at my wrist, to the miniature screen there, confirms it. My dad is calling me at seven on a Thursday. Wrong day, wrong time.

A little voice whispers in the back of my head to ignore it. Its once inescapable thrum had gone quiet for years, dormant. Now something has brought it back.

I ignore the voice, knowing putting this off will only make it worse, and accept the call. "Dad." My voice is hoarse.

"Paul," he answers, sounding mildly surprised at first. He clears his throat and it disappears. "Glad I caught you." My dad hesitates then, torn on what to say next, though it's clear this call came with a specific purpose. It's unusual for him not to be direct, to the point of discomfort sometimes. The pit in my stomach stretches wider as I go to the locker room to grab a towel from the shelf.

If he thinks I'm going to urge him forward, fill the silence, he's mistaken. I might answer his weekly calls, schedule my life around them—build my life around what he believes in—but every rare moment when he's caught off guard like this is a small victory for me. For the voice in the back of my head I thought had gone dormant.

"How have things been? Everything good at work?" he finally asks when we're already past the border of awkward.

"Fine, good. Look, Dad, I'm actually at the gym right now," I offer, hoping it might bring this to an end sooner. He doesn't need to know I've finished my workout.

This seems to jumpstart things. "Right, I won't keep you then. Your cousin sent your mother a video." He stops, probably for dramatic effect, and the urge to scoff rears up in me like a horse on its hind legs. "Of you."

My legs quiver and it's a longer way down to the small bench in the men's locker room than I thought, the backs of my thighs slapping against the unyielding wood when I sit. I knew this was possible, that the whole point of this project was to be seen, but I thought I'd have more time before it reached my family. Our videos haven't been getting a lot of traction yet.

Taking a deep breath, I decide the best course of action is to cork this off at the source. "Dad, it's not what you think—"

"I'm not entirely sure what I think," he cuts me off, and it sounds like he's trying to force a laugh on the other end of that line. "Are you switching careers on me?"

Of course that's what he'd be worried about. "No, nothing like that. I got pulled into a project for a product launch. They need to keep it under budget." I know that vague explanation probably wouldn't make sense to the average outsider, but it's speaking right to my dad's heart. Budgets and numbers: his love language.

It seems to satisfy him. "Ah, they're skimping on the cost of actors by putting in the finance guy?" The first word comes out like a chuckle and relief floods my veins. Then I'm angry at myself for still caring so much what this man thinks of me. Like it's in my DNA to seek his favor.

Maybe it is.

Desperate to get off the phone before I say something I'll regret, I force a chuckle of my own. "Yep, you got it. It's only for a few weeks. On top of my normal duties." I add the last part to head off any further questions.

I know it did the trick when I hear my father blow out a long breath, the signal of a conversation coming to a close. "Well, don't work too hard. Unless it'll get you a promotion." He laughs stiffly at his joke while I pinch the bridge of my nose between my thumb and forefinger.

I can't click the button to end the call fast enough, a strange blend of rage and fear taking root in my chest like it always does when we dance around it. My past. Our past. The thing we don't discuss anymore.

Not a thing, I remind myself, looking down at the phone still in my hand like I can see the unanswered invitation buried in it. Not *just* a thing.

When I disable Do Not Disturb mode, a text message from my cousin Bethany pops up. The first word is in all caps: SORRY! It's followed by a brief explanation, a link, and another apology.

Ah. Well, at least she'd tried to warn me.

The link opens a social media app on my phone—I'd been forced against my will to download it and make an account for this project—and auto plays a video of... *oh*.

When our first recipe video bombed, I had reservations about doing another, but no idea how to broach the subject with Cate. The apple cocktail had been her idea. Her baby. I'd already stepped on her toes once recently and couldn't afford another round of the silent treatment in this partnership.

After that one did almost as poorly, she'd agreed we should experiment with something else. Enter: the frothing incident. My frothing incident. I knew this was coming, had agreed to post it this week, but somehow blocked out the fact that this one might have different results.

I can't help but smile a little when I see it has over ten thousand views and a hundred comments. It might be embarrassing, but it's doing what we'd hoped for.

When I expand the comments and start reading though, I wince. The top one says "I've never been so jealous of a kitchen tool." Seems innocent enough, until I keep reading. The next one down is even worse: "TBH I'd explode everywhere too if that guy was holding me." *What the heck?*

Cringing, I hold the phone a full arm's length away, like I can put some distance between myself and the commenters. The last one I see says "Raw. Next question," whatever that means. And it must mean something, because it has over a hundred likes.

Are these people talking about me? On one hand, I think these comments are complimentary. But on the other hand, they make me feel a little dirty.

Oh god, and my parents saw these!

I feel like I might collapse into a puddle on the locker room floor. I guess it's the best place for it since I'll wash right down the drain.

Why Bethany thought it was a good idea to send this to my mom, I will never understand. She owes me big time.

CHAPTER 12

Paul

YESTERDAY MORNING, THERE WERE two liters of lemon-lime soda in my bottom desk drawer when I arrived to work. Now, I know what you're picturing: I pull out the drawer, the largest one in my desk's three-tiered filing cabinet, to find all my folders replaced with two large, green plastic bottles raucously bouncing against one another from the sliding motion. That's what any sane person would imagine.

No. That's not what happened at all. I opened my desk drawer to dig for the balance sheets from last quarter and instead my hand got wet. Without looking—because why would I need to? I've repeated this motion one thousand times without issue—I slid the drawer out and reached for my forest-green-dyed manila folders, all hanging in an orderly row. Instead of finding the thick, fibrous paper, my fingers plunged into bubbly liquid. *Room temperature* bubbly liquid. It was like being shoved into an episode of *Fear Factor*.

How did this happen, you ask? In the exact way you'd expect: Cate Seymour poured at least five cans of VitaPop's *Limony-Snicket* soda into my bottom desk drawer.

And that's not even the most surprising part of this entire situation. I *smiled*. Fingertips still dripping with soda, my lips had the audacity to curve.

What's the opposite of personal growth? Personal going backward? Whatever it is, these last few weeks with Cate have done it to me.

I'm not complaining, exactly. I've laughed more times in fourteen days than I think I have in the past two years. We discovered that our audience isn't interested in polished content. After some trial and error, we managed to go semi-viral three times, and each time was when we either screwed something up—like me with the stupid frother—or did something completely asinine.

Like making a Barbie-sized soda pool out of my desk drawer, complete with miniature floaties and palm trees affixed to the corners with tape. At least she had the good sense to remove my folders first. Otherwise I'd have a hard time explaining to our CEO why I couldn't locate the hard copy of last year's P&L's for his meeting with the executive committee today.

My personal favorite had been our attempt to make apple pie with our haul from the orchard, but replacing the butter and water with apple soda. It fizzed over so much in the oven it took us over an hour to clean up the resulting mess. We caught the entire eruption on camera, though, which made it all worth it.

If I had to guess, Cate's favorite was the time she used three jalapeños to make me a spicy apple mock-a-rita. She didn't even seed the damn things. It was like drinking from a hot tub in hell. I ended up chugging the entire container of vanilla creamer we had left over from our first video shoot to cool my taste buds. It was disgusting and I may have burned off the top layer of my tongue altogether, but it worked. That one got almost twenty thousand views.

Being with Cate is easier than I expected. Not quite *easy*, but a far cry from difficult, considering our rocky start. That history, it keeps us at arm's length. We let ourselves get just comfortable enough to do the job well, but go no further. She doesn't ask the hard questions, doesn't pry into topics I'd rather not discuss, and I offer her the same courtesy in return.

I'd spent so long thinking a true friendship wasn't something I could have after Jake. Eventually the surface-level stuff wouldn't be enough. They'd want to know who I am, and to do that, they'd need to know who I was. Why I couldn't be that person anymore.

But all Cate has demanded of me so far is the surface-level, and I've been only too eager to give it to her.

My eyes drift to the cheap clock hanging on my otherwise bare apartment wall. It's a Walmart special, left behind by the previous renter, with a plain white face and a thick black frame made from plastic so thin that it practically falls apart when you look at it. And right now it shows Cate is thirty minutes late.

Contrary to my expectations when we started this ill-fated partnership, Cate is never late. On time for her is at least three minutes early, but usually more. She'd warned me her rugby games can be unpredictable, but she'd promised to text me an update by four. That would be plenty of time, she'd said, the game long over by then.

As the second hand of the clock rounds the bases once more, I can feel each tick against the side of my brain. It's now 4:31, and not a single peep from her. I tap the glass screen of my phone to light it up, confirming no notifications slipped through my watchful eye in the past minute.

Nothing greets me except the same screen saver I've had for three phones and nearly a decade: a stunning view of a sea-glass lake from high atop a peak in the Bavarian Alps so green you'd think it's been edited. A sliver from my old life carried over to my new one. A small piece I couldn't bring myself to erase.

By the time my watch shows five, I'm pacing my apartment. It reminds me how small the place is. I can barely get twelve steps in before I need to turn around and begin again. *It would barely contain Cate*, I think to myself, eyes sweeping the entirety of its shoebox size. The living room is smaller than my freshman dorm in college, barely enough space for a loveseat and television.

The kitchen is no better. I can't open the oven door all the way without it scraping the little cart that serves as a makeshift island opposite it. Good thing I don't cook much.

She'd take two steps in and laugh. Not the sniff she does when she's pretending something's amusing, a polite but fleeting sound meant to humor you, but the earth-shattering cackle she reserves only for the things she finds truly funny. When I turn back around to take the next twelve paces, my lips are spread in a smile.

"This is where you live?!" she'd cry, her voice bouncing against the plain white walls. "I've seen hamster cages bigger than this."

I chuckle darkly and look at the clock on the microwave, so close it's visible clearly from the living room. Five fifteen now, it says. That's it, I can't take it anymore. She can make fun of me all she wants, but at least I'll know what's going on.

I grab my phone from the island and shoot her a quick message: **Is your game over?**

No response.

I try sitting on my miniature sofa, ankle over knee, but my foot keeps bouncing of its own accord, making my entire body shake. The old beige cushions sag even more than usual from the vibration. This time I wait only seven more minutes before firing off another text: `Did you still want to film today?`

Simple, to the point, not overly concerned.

Because I'm not concerned. A sound between a laugh and a scoff escapes the back of my throat when I throw my phone back down on the couch. I'm not concerned at all. It's just that she's now more than an hour late for our meeting and it's rude. Made even more so by the fact that she hasn't texted me to tell me why she's late in the first place. Or when she'll be ready to meet me at the test kitchen.

You know what, two can play that game. I flip my phone over so it's face down on the couch and turn my head in the opposite direction, suddenly interested in the mysterious crack in the wall beside the light switch. How did it get there? Was it from me, when I first moved in, or left behind by an old tenant?

Couldn't have been me. I'd remember.

Maybe whoever used to live here was having a party one night, a daring feat given the size of this place, and someone knocked into it during a particularly rowdy game of beer pong. Or maybe they had simply been trying to hang a photo of a loved one they missed when the nail split the drywall in two.

My mouth dries, a parched feeling I can't swallow down, and I grab for my phone again. It's been only thirteen more minutes, and I groan my exasperation at its too-bright screen.

My mouth twists to one side, chest heaving up and down with my breaths. What if something happened to her? I don't know much about rugby, but I imagine it's a lot like football. Could she have gotten hurt? Or perhaps it was a car accident afterward; so overcome with her victory, she didn't even see the other vehicle coming.

Or maybe she'd been trying to text me, one hand on her phone, the other on the wheel, all of her attention on the message she was typing, when another car came barreling out of nowhere.

My throat constricts. I feel like one of those old-timey cartoons the way my heart pounds against the inside of my chest cavity, like it should be visible through my bones, skin, and clothing.

Before I know what I'm doing, my car keys are in my hand, my brown suede jacket only halfway tugged onto one arm while I race down the narrow stairs of my apartment building. I've only been to her place once—not to visit, only to pick her up on the way to film when her car was at the mechanic's—but muscle memory takes over, showing me the way.

I haven't thought about what I'll say when I get there. What I'll do if she's not there. All I can focus on is staying on the road, and then finding a parking spot. Climbing out the driver's side of my Subaru and slamming the car door a little harder than I mean to. Racing up the sidewalk to the little white house with the sky-blue shutters and the cracked bottom step.

The doorbell is broken, she told me before, so I knock. Hard. No, firmly. I'm still in control here, a well-meaning colleague who needs to know if his Saturday night freed up or not.

"*Cate*," I breathe when she answers the door wearing a pair of pale purple cotton shorts and a white tank top. She's cradling a Ziploc bag to her head with one hand.

I must look a little wilder than I realize, because her mouth pulls to one side—the little rosebud that means she's thinking. "Paul, what are you doing here?"

"I uh." I cough into a fist, spine going straight. "I texted you a few times."

Her face drains of color. Well, what little color it has, which isn't as much as I'm used to. "But I texted you earlier, told you I..." She looks into the quiet house behind her, gesturing with her free hand like she's reaching for something.

My eyes widen at the same time her shoulders curl in on themselves. "I didn't get any messages from you, Cate," I explain softly, wincing when the plastic bag she holds against her head slips.

"Wait here," she tells me, running deeper into the house. When she reemerges, she's staring at her phone screen in mute horror.

"I'm so sorry, Paul. I tried to text you hours ago to cancel, but it looks like it never sent."

When she looks back up at me, she must notice the way my eyes flicker to and from the Ziploc bag a few times, because she pulls it away from her head and holds it forward. "Ice pack. I took a hit during the game today. That's why I couldn't meet you." She's frowning, her hazel eyes round and shiny. Apologetic, I realize, and maybe a little worried.

"To your head?" I ask as calmly as I can. The well of fear that's been dormant inside me for years almost doesn't take notice. *Almost*.

She nods and then winces sharply, placing the ice pack back where it was, resting on the side of her temple. A bandage to hold together an invisible wound. And there it is, the floodgates lift, the wave crests through me so ferociously there's nothing I can do but roll with the tide.

I rush forward in a panic, grasping her under an elbow to lead her back inside. "Come on, you need to sit down." Without a clue where I'm going, I manage to guide her to a crowded, rectangular living room, bedecked in all the hues of the rainbow, like I knew it would be after seeing her desk at work.

Ordinarily, a place like this would send me into a mini spiral. Too many colors in too small an area. Too visually loud. Overstimulated, that's the latest buzzword describing it, the anxiety it brings on.

Instead, I feel laser-focused, my attention split only between my mission to find a place to sit and the soft warmth of Cate's elbow in my hand.

Control. Control and care will get us through this.

With my help, she takes a slow seat on a plush couch the color of poppies in full bloom, resting her back against a pillow with a dog's portrait stamped on it four times, Andy Warhol-style.

"Can I get you anything? Water? Aspirin?" Cautiously, I take a seat next to her, my hands still hovering near her arms as though she might break if I back off completely. For the first time, I notice a red mark on her bare collarbones and my nostrils flare. How many other marks and scars and bruises does she bare?

She's always worn them with pride, the few I noticed here and there at the office. A stiff jaw, battle scars on display for the world to see, a sign that the small hurts meant nothing to her. They couldn't bring her down.

But now, watching her stiffly adjust herself on the sofa and then wince after moving the wrong way, cradling a makeshift ice pack to her head, it's different. For the first time, she looks frail. Breakable.

"Water would be nice, thank you." She closes her eyes, settling into a position that doesn't make her forehead crease with pain.

CHAPTER 13

Cate

PAUL ANDREWS IS FUMBLING around in my kitchen. He must open every cabinet in there until he finds the one with the water glasses.

If you had told me four weeks ago that this is where I'd be today, I would've laughed in your face. And possibly pressured you into being evaluated by a licensed professional. I'm still a little shocked myself, but I opened the door and let him rush me inside, set me on the couch. A physical manifestation of how much our relationship has changed.

The strange look on his face when I'd first opened the door had shaken me. It was one I'd never seen him wear before. As soon as I realized what I'd done, panic had set in. How could I forget to push send on my text? Why didn't I double—no, triple!—check to make sure he got it? No, I'd put my phone on Do Not Disturb because looking at the screen made my eyes hurt and plopped down on the sofa.

I pride myself on my professionalism, and this is not the impression I want to leave on a colleague, even one I despise. Or used to despise. After my confession, I'd eyed him carefully, searching for the look of disapproval he always wore so well around the office. Around me.

Instead, he looked wild. His jaw was slack instead of hardened steel, his chest heaving with every breath. He'd looked like he'd seen a ghost. And maybe that's what I look like right now, a ghost. What little makeup I put on before the game has probably rubbed off by now, my threadbare pajamas are on, and there's a half-eaten bag of frozen peas and carrots stuck to the side of my head with nothing but a thin layer of plastic storage bag between my skin and its opening.

On second thought, he was probably grossed out when he saw me.

Well, whatever, I think, keeping my eyes shut. Even the dim auburn light cast by the lamp in the corner with the red scarf tossed over its shade is a little too much. At least I'd managed a half-assed shower before he showed up here unannounced. I wince, this time not from pain. He did say he texted me a few times, didn't he? *Oops. Damn you, Do Not Disturb!*

I'd been a little preoccupied, you know, getting checked for signs of a concussion. Fortunately, the doctor at the urgent care didn't think I had one, but my head still feels as if a parade of bears in tutus are doing the cha-cha inside it.

The sound of a cabinet door shutting and water pouring into a glass drifts in from the kitchen. Though I'd sooner lay down on train tracks than admit it, I'm sort of glad Paul showed up. Mindy's spending the night at her boyfriend's so I've got the whole house to myself. She offered to cancel her plans, stay with me, but that felt childish to ask. Selfish.

I'd thought about calling home, but there's no way I could ask my mom to hop on a plane from southern California to, what? Watch me lay on the sofa? I know how that conversation ends.

Maybe if it had been a playoff game and she was already here, with Dad. If they'll even come this time. My breath rattles in my lungs, and I shift on the couch.

It's not like I need help anyway. I was getting along fine here by myself. But I don't totally hate the idea of company, even if it is Paul Andrews. And the look of concern he wore when he asked if I needed anything... I'd be lying if I said he didn't wear it well.

Paul returns, triumphantly brandishing a glass of water like it's the Holy Grail. I can't help but smile through the pain that rocks me when I sit up to accept it. In an instant his self-satisfied grin is replaced by a frown. He gently pushes me back with one hand on my shoulder and lifts the cup to my lips with the other, like he's going to feed it to me. Or whatever the beverage equivalent of that is.

I blink at him, biting my bottom lip to keep from snickering, and force myself to a reclined position. When I extend a hand for the glass, I say as gently as I can, "I think I can handle a sip of water."

A flush creeps across his cheeks and he nods, letting me take the cup from him. Our fingertips brush during the exchange, and he pulls away quickly.

After I take a slow gulp from the glass, I reach forward to set it on the coffee table. Hesitantly, Paul takes a seat beside me on the couch, folding his hands in his lap. He looks too big for it. An adult sitting on children's furniture. I'm so used to seeing Mindy's willowy frame there instead.

For a few moments, we sit in silence, nothing to keep us company but the low hum of an old BBC show set in the fictional kingdom of Camelot playing in the background. Thank god for Mindy's parents and their Prime Video account.

Caught up in an episode I've seen before, I almost forget Paul's there, until I hear him sniff a laugh under his breath then cough to hide it.

"Have you seen this show?" I ask, watching him from the corner of my eye.

"No," he answers, and I roll my lips together. "But it's pretty funny," he adds quickly, and one corner of my mouth tugs up. That reflex to smooth things over with me, it started in our first meeting together. At the time, I didn't think much of it. Our partnership was awkward at best and he, like any rational person, wanted to make it less so. But it's only seemed to grow since the incident at the orchard. I can't say I mind.

We watch the episode together in silence again, the prince getting himself into trouble and his servant with hidden powers helping him escape it, leaving the former none-the-wiser, as usual. When it breaks for the next episode, I feel Paul's eyes on my face.

"How—" He hesitates, clearing his throat into his closed hand. "What happened?" His voice breaks on the final syllable, stirring a strange feeling in my gut.

In no rush, I tilt my head to look at him and shrug. "I took a hit in the game today." The same thing I'd told him at the door. I know it's not the explanation he wants, but the old me is still in here and I can't help tease him a bit.

His eyes narrow and *there's* the look of disapproval I'd been look-ing for earlier. Only now instead of fearing it, I want to bathe in it.

It hurts to hold back my laugh. I tilt my head back against the sofa, a plush pink throw blanket draped there cushioning me. "Without boring you with the details, I'm a forward. Specifically an openside flanker."

I pause to see if he's following and though I'm sure I've lost him already, the intensity of his focus encourages me to keep going. "Basically I try to get the ball if we don't have it and I protect our possession of the ball when we do. So I get tackled. A lot. And do a lot of tackling too. This time, it was the former."

His eyebrows jerk up. "You play a sport that pummels you to the ground frequently on purpose?"

This time I can't hold back the laugh, though it comes out choked. "You say that like we're out there beating on each other."

"Are you not?"

"No! There's way more to it than that. Besides, no one bats an eye when a guy says he plays football." I cock an eyebrow at him and he winces.

"Fair point. For most people. Personally, I never gave a shit about football." He doesn't realize he's sworn until my mouth pops open in awe. Then all the color in his face floods to his temples, his forehead turning bright red.

"What sports do you like?" I ask, because I can't help it.

He lifts and drops one shoulder. "I ran cross-country in high school, if that counts?"

"It doesn't," I say to get a reaction out of him, though I don't mean it.

One corner of his mouth twitches and the sight of it dulls some of the pain in my head.

Ignoring my jab, he continues on, "I never really watched sports unless it was with my dad. Football, try as I might, I couldn't get into with him. Soccer wasn't half bad, I guess."

For a few seconds I watch him, sensing there's more. When I've waited him out long enough, he adds, "I preferred hiking to any of it. Cross-country scratched the itch half-way, because at least I got to spend time outside. But the courses weren't... challenging enough. Eventually, I quit and started hiking more on my own." A shadow passes over his face, there and gone in a flash.

I don't even have the time to process it, because something else he said caught my attention. Paul Andrews, a quitter? It's a far cry from the picture of him I've painted in my head these last few years.

Then again, so is just about everything I've witnessed the past few weeks.

"So why do you do it?" he interrupts.

Shooting him a confused look, I uncurl my legs from beneath me to stretch out the growing cramp in my right calf. If I keep my toes flexed toward the ceiling and my back flush against the armrest on this side of the couch, there's barely enough room to extend my legs fully without touching his thigh. Only now I'm hyper-fixated on his thigh and have completely forgotten what he asked that had me confused in the first place.

"Why rugby?" he elaborates and I hum.

This could be either a simple answer, or an extremely complicated one. It would be so easy to brush it off. He'd let it go too. Maybe because he wouldn't pick up on my tell, that I'm hiding something. But something tells me he would, and he'd let me get away with it anyway.

"My older brother played football," I begin, kneading my fingers into the fleshy part of my calf. "He was good. Great, even. The only sophomore to start varsity at our school. Made it to the playoffs every year he played, and even won state twice." My mind drifts to that shelf full of trophies in the den, shelves filled with his achievements.

I don't begrudge them, or him. He earned them, had every right to display his victories proudly. To be celebrated.

I only wanted some of it for myself too. To have a place there beside him, an equal.

Keeping my gaze trained in the middle distance, I go on. "My parents went to every single one of his games, even the ones that were hours away. They drove, or bought seats on the booster club bus to ride with all the other football parents." I swallow, and my eyes find Paul's. Even though it's dark outside my window and there's barely any light coming from the heavily-veiled lamp in the corner, I find them.

"I wanted that," I admit quietly, and it feels good to say it out loud for what might be the first time. The only person in Seattle who knows even a small part of this is Mindy, and I was forced to tell her about my strained relationship with my family when she wondered why they almost never come to visit.

"I must've tried every single sport they had, first in the youth athletic association and then in middle and high school." Twisting my mouth to one side to bite on my cheek, my eyes flash. "I was terrible at all of them."

"No," Paul breathes and even though I didn't know it before, it's exactly the reaction I wanted. Disbelief. Adamant rejection of the idea that I, Cate Seymour, could possibly fail at something. It's like it gives me permission to be honest. To be me.

I can't help but grin. "Oh yeah, awful. Field hockey? If I wasn't tripping over my own stick, then I was doing it to my teammates. Soccer was far too much running around aimlessly, so you can imagine how I felt about track—"

He snorts, and I kick his leg lightly then let my foot rest there, barely touching him. He doesn't flinch, doesn't try to move away. In fact, he relaxes into it, and it's as if a dam breaks in my chest, the weight I've carried all these years leaking out of me.

"Pretty soon, I think my parents gave up on me. My younger sister started cheerleading and they had someone else to focus on when Brian went off to college." There were practices every day, games every weekend, competitions four times a year. Plenty enough to keep them busy. I shrug, even as my sinuses start to ache and I feel that telltale prickle behind my eyes. There's no turning back though, I've already made it this far.

"I gave up for a while too, focused on my grades instead. I thought maybe that could be my thing. I could be the smart one." I try to smile through this, but it doesn't reach my eyes. Unfortunately, there are no bleachers in the classroom. No booster club bus for the SATs. No jerseys for turning in your homework. "It was great for me, gave me access to any college of my choosing. But I still felt like it wasn't enough."

Paul clenches his jaw tight, like he's trying to keep from opening his mouth. It makes me wonder what he'd say, if he let himself. And maybe it's because I've already showed him one of the darkest parts of myself, the secret room no one else is allowed to enter, but I stretch my foot again until it's nestled completely against his leg. Until there's no mistaking that I did it on purpose.

I watch as his hand, the one resting on top of his thigh, flexes like it wants to move, but isn't sure it should. He balls it into a fist, flattens it back out again. Then, as though it's pulled by a magnetic force beyond his control, it begins to move. Inch by inch. Until it comes to sit on top of my foot. His thumb sweeps a soft stroke against the inside of my arch, then presses down, a gentle nudge that he's here, that he wants me to keep going.

My throat feels tight now and it's hard to focus on anything but the feel of his hand on me, the warmth of his skin. "My roommate at UW played rugby and convinced me to join the club team," I rasp and reach for the cup of water Paul brought me, still half full on the coffee table. I take a long gulp before continuing. "I told her it was a waste of time, that I was no athlete. Turns out I just hadn't found the right sport."

"Naturally you'd be most gifted at the violent one," Paul teases in a small voice, and a barking laugh sneaks out of me like a thief in the night. Totally unexpected.

"Right? Apparently I should've tried out for the football team back then. Maybe I'd have given my brother a run for his money."

"Do your parents come to your games now?" It's such an innocent question, something any normal person would ask next, one I should've prepared for. Instead, it leaves me reeling, mouth hanging open like an idiot.

"They... We haven't..." I stammer, searching for an explanation, an excuse. "It's pretty far for them," I land on after a few moments. "They live in a small town north of LA. They'd basically have to fly here to make it." I force a laugh, like that would be preposterous to even request. It comes out more like a hacking cough, and I quickly cover my mouth with my hand.

He doesn't need to know that I've asked, many times, and they've turned me down. Made excuses. That they've only been inside this house one time before, right after I moved in. Only came to one of my games at UW.

As talented as I became on the field, I guess it wasn't enough for them.

Paul nods, his fingertips now drawing absentminded circles on the inside of my ankle. Like that first touch made a crack in the wall between us, the big one that says *Hey, you guys are colleagues!*, and now more bricks are starting to crumble. It's doing very dangerous things to my insides, but I welcome the distraction. Revel in it, even.

"Well, if you ever want someone to show up to a game in one of those rainbow-colored wigs and foam fingers, say the word. I know a guy."

Something about the casual way he throws it out there, like he'd give up any afternoon or evening, cancel plans he already made to come watch me, like it's nothing. Something about the way his fingers are both hot and cold against my skin at the same time, how they know exactly where to knead and push and stroke, like they were made to touch me. It snaps something loose in me. I can hear it, a thunderclap echoing in my skull, the sound so real and loud I wonder if he can hear it too.

And then I'm on top of him.

CHAPTER 14

Paul

CATE SEYMOUR TASTES LIKE strawberries fresh from the vine. My mom kept a small garden of them when I was a kid, just for me. Every summer—until I reached that age when a teenage boy wants nothing to do with his family—I'd sneak outside while she washed the dinner dishes and pluck them, one by one, popping them into my mouth. They would be warm from the sun, the juice more sweet than tart when it exploded into my mouth.

And that is exactly what Cate tastes like.

For a moment, it's all I can think about. It drowns out the questions, the ones I don't want to answer. The ones that beg me to stop and think about what we're doing, the line we're crossing.

I block them out, focusing instead of how I feel. How *she* feels. Her lips are soft when they part for me and I suck her lower lip into my mouth, eager. I don't have time to wonder how we got here. I can't question my good fortune, not when she's straddling my thighs and tasting me with her tongue.

I brace my hands around her waist, pulling her down until our hips are flush. She makes a tiny whimpering sound in the back of her throat and I pull back, enough to see her. "Are you okay? Did I hurt you?" My eyes flick to her temple while one of my hands slides up her back. She abandoned the frozen veggies right before she lunged for me, and I fear the peas and carrots may be rolling across her carpet.

She smiles and answers me with another kiss. Silences me is more like it, but that attitude of hers is growing on me.

After yanking my sweater over my head, she tosses it over her shoulder and roves her cool hands across my bare torso. It makes me grateful for the fitness regimen my father drilled into me from a young age. Then I'm annoyed with myself for thinking about my dad and the gym right now when Cate is right here, nibbling on my lip, unbuttoning my jeans.

At some point, we migrate to her bedroom, my fly completely undone so I have to waddle a bit to keep my pants from falling down on the trek. When we get there, it takes every ounce of willpower I have not to unceremoniously leave Cate on her bed and snoop around instead.

My work-enemy-turned-friend's bedroom. What might I find in here? What else could I learn about her? Guilt bleeds into my thoughts and I pull up short, breaking our kiss for the second time.

Cate still doesn't know me, not fully. I haven't told her my secret. The biggest thing there is to know about me, the thing that set my life on its trajectory. Or bumped me off of the old trajectory, depending on how you look at it.

Sensing my hesitation, she draws back, then winces. Her thighs are still spread across my lap when she lifts a gentle hand to the side of her head.

"Your injury," I say, frowning in its direction. It's not quite a question and not quite a full statement either.

She understands anyway and smiles sheepishly. "Maybe we should slow this down. Until I'm whole again." Her mouth twists to one side, that little rosebud popping into existence. Her thinking face. "Is that okay?"

Instead of answering immediately, I first press a featherlight kiss to the tip of her nose. Her shoulders slump, relief mixed with a little disappointment to end things, perhaps?

After one more chaste kiss to her lips, I move to slide her off of me. "I can leave and let you get some rest."

Cate squeezes her thighs even tighter around mine. A restraint. "Could you... stay?"

I don't think I've ever seen her look so vulnerable, not even earlier when she confessed to me about her family, her fears of being left out. I can't fathom the courage it probably took her to ask me. It squeezes my chest, makes it hard not to start things up again.

My small smile turns lopsided and I slide my fingertips through her blonde hair. It's curled at the ends now, like she recently ran through a sprinkler and let it air dry in the sun. "I would love to," I whisper, my breath tickling her lips.

Neither of us brings up what this means for our quickly evolving relationship. Seems we're both content to let that ball hang in the air for now.

CHAPTER 15

Cate

THE DIAL TONE IS too loud with the phone sandwiched between my ear and shoulder, but I need both my hands to unlock my car and toss my bag of gear into the passenger seat. My heart hammers, an unsteady racing beat. It reminds me of the time I pushed myself too hard on the treadmill in college and nearly blacked out.

Calling my parents should not give me a heart attack, but here we are.

"Hi sweetie, this is unexpected," my mom says when she picks up. To some, this might sound totally innocuous. Maybe even loving. A parental figure who desperately misses their child, wishes they'd reach out more. But in my mom's tone, all I find is mild irritation disguised behind polite words.

Trying to keep my voice chipper, I apologize for catching her off guard, then immediately regret it. Why should I apologize for calling home once in a blue moon? Already this is off on the wrong foot and I haven't made it past the greeting. *Get your head in the game, Seymour.*

When I switch my car on, a tan Nissan Rogue that still runs well despite being almost half my age, the call transfers to the speakers and I drop my phone into a cup holder. "Remember when we talked about you and Dad coming to visit sometime soon?"

I purse my lips, waiting. After what feels like an eternity, she says, "A little bit, yeah."

While my left hand braces against the steering wheel, the right falls into my lap, and I fiddle with the ring on my index finger, using my thumb to twist it around in circles. Cool, this isn't going to be easy. I shift the car into drive and plow on. "How does two weeks from now sound?"

There's a rustling on the other end of the line and I can picture my mom pulling out her paper calendar. Even as I want to roll my eyes, it brings a small smile to my lips. She swears if she doesn't write it down, it will disappear. *My appointments are always getting lost on that iPhone.* Yeah, probably because you never save them right.

"Oh, I don't know honey. It's a little short notice." More rustling and then silence when she reaches the right page. "Your sister has a home game that day."

She says this with the plaintive tone of someone who works for the NFL and just got invited to an amateur bowling tournament the same day as the Super Bowl. You'd never guess she's talking about seeing her daughter wave some pompoms, for the hundredth time, at a UCLA football game.

Even though I knew it was coming, my stomach sinks. I clench my jaw to keep from saying something I'll regret, like "The Bruins are having a terrible season so there's not much for her to cheer for anyway."

Through gritted teeth, I release my proverbial ace in the hole. "My rugby team made it to the championships. Officially cinched our spot in today's playoff game. I thought maybe you and Dad could come watch me play."

Even with my small injury in the mix, we'd won our last four games in a row. Tomorrow, the last two teams left in the bracket will face off, and we'll play the winner in the final.

"Hello?" I ask after a pause, tapping my phone screen while stopped at a red light to see if the call disconnected. My left leg is bouncing up and down in an uneven rhythm, making the car vibrate.

"I'm sorry, honey," my mom answers, and right away I know she's not apologizing for the brief silence. I shift my weight back in the car's bucket seat and try to keep my sigh inaudible.

"It would be a lot to organize at the last minute, and your dad's been working a lot of overtime now that everyone's out of the house. We can't make it happen."

Not even an "I'll try" or "Let me talk to your dad" or "I'll see if I can move some things around." It's a done deal from the start.

"Can't" really means "won't" here, but I've gone the past twenty-six years without saying these intrusive thoughts out loud. Why start now? I lick my lips as the light turns green and follow the car ahead of me through the intersection, squinting at the sun refracting off its bright white paint. It's definitely not because of the tears pricking at the back of my eyes.

I can't help but wonder: If it had been Brian reaching out, would the outcome of this conversation be different? If my little sister wasn't cheering at a college game that day, would my parents make an effort? If I'd been better at sports as a kid, or done something differently, something to make them love me more, would it have changed anything? The sinking feeling in my gut tells me what I don't want to admit.

"Of course, I understand," I rasp, already reaching for the button to end the call. My hand trembles and it takes me a few tries before I get it. The car becomes a vacuum of silence, leaving me with nothing but the tingling in my chest and the numbness in my limbs to keep me company. I can't even muster up the energy to put on the radio.

No matter how many times I say I understand, I fear I never will.

CHAPTER 16

Paul

"FINALLY! I WAS STARTING to think you were dodging me," I tease into the phone after throwing my car in park. I just made the twenty-minute drive to Cate's house for a glamorous Friday night filled with all my favorite things: data, spreadsheets, and greasy Chinese food, when my lovely cousin Bethany deigned to return my calls.

"I am so sorry! I will never forgive myself for not checking with you first. I assumed they knew!" Bethany cries without preamble, though I can hear the amusement in her voice. "Tony's Trattoria. All the pizza, pasta, and beer you can consume, on me. Name the date."

I grin at my windshield, the world beyond it turning from hazy pink to charcoal gray. These late September sunsets keep coming earlier and earlier. Pretty soon it will be dark before Cate and I even leave the office. "Ah, is that why you called? Trying to bribe me back into your good graces?"

Bethany doesn't have to bribe me and she knows it. She's probably my favorite person in the whole world. *Second favorite?* I shake my head and blink the question away.

"Actually, I called to see if you were heading back to Eugene." She pauses and I can hear the gears whirring in her brain, searching for the missing part of her sentence. The part she doesn't want to say. The part only she could get away with saying. "For Mrs. Turner's thing," is what she settles on.

My grin slips and I'm thankful she can't see me. The truth is, I haven't thought about it. Okay, that's a lie—I have thought about it. I haven't *wanted* to think about it, so I've tried everything in my power to avoid it completely. It's gotten so bad that I won't even look at my phone most nights, unless I'm expecting a text from Cate. It's one of the (very small) reasons I've loved spending so much time with her these past few weeks. It usually starts out with work, a video we need to film or ideas we need to brainstorm and finesse. But then it almost always turns into something else, the two of us simply existing together. Those parts are my favorite.

"It's just, I thought we could carpool," Bethany adds when I've been quiet for too long.

"I'm not sure," I hedge, dragging my teeth across my bottom lip, searching for a better excuse. "I got pulled into a big project at work unexpectedly and I'm burning the midnight oil more than usual. I need to see if I can move some things around first." It's thin and she'll probably see right through it. She knows me better than anyone. The upside is she knows me well enough to accept it. To let me work through this in my own time.

There's a false brightness to her tone when she responds, "Okay! Well, if you decide to go, hit me up. I promise not to dodge you this time." She laughs and it's only half real, but I appreciate the subject change nonetheless.

With a smile that doesn't quite reach my eyes, I say, "Of course. And I'm holding you to that promise—all-you-can-eat Tony's."

"Looking forward to it," she says, and she sounds a little more like her usual self this time, the false cheer gone. *It's okay*, it says. She understands.

We hang up, and I grab my work bag from the passenger seat then climb out of my car, stretching my legs and back a little before crossing the deserted street to Cate's house. She greets me at the door, wearing a small smile, a pair of black leggings that hug her every curve, and a cropped slate gray T-shirt that says "BEAST BEAUTY BRAINS" in all capital letters. It's like it was made for her.

She beckons me in with an erratic wave, and I tell her I already ordered our takeout on the way over and it should be here in fifteen minutes. It's my fourth time at her house, but I still wait for her to invite me to sit down beside her on the couch.

"You're so formal," she teases around a straw stuffed into a can of VitaPop cola.

I take my seat, crossing my ankles under the coffee table in front of the couch. "I prefer polite. Considerate. Charming. An extraordinary gentleman." Joking with her has become as involuntary as breathing.

She sniffs a laugh and pulls her laptop from the table into her lap. "Okay, monthly reports go out Monday and I want to wow Darius with our results so far." She pulls up a spreadsheet she started at work today and walks me through it, the red nail polish she wears flashing each time she points something out.

I try to look at the screen, to concentrate, but it's hard to focus on anything but her. Our campaign has been doing better than we'd initially projected after our rocky start, and her excitement is palpable in the air. If I stuck my tongue out, I could taste it. Sugared flower petals and pop rocks.

She's beautiful on a regular day. Her rosebud lips that always have a little pink in them, her hazel eyes that change color in bright sunlight, the way the muscles in her arms or legs ripple when she moves. I have to physically restrain myself around her at the office sometimes, especially when she wears that damn brown corduroy skirt. It's like now that I've gotten a taste, however small, I'm fiending for more.

Now though, when she's talking about something she loves and her speech is coming just a little too fast, her eyes are dancing in the glow from the small lamps littering her living room, and there's a flush the shade of a carnation creeping across her cheeks? It's ethereal.

Not even the allure of Excel sheets in need of a good formatting can tear me away. I'm staring at her. The part of my brain that stores all the social cues I've learned over a lifetime, the manners, the *how-to-politely-behave-in-company* guides, has disappeared.

Fortunately for me, the doorbell rings after a few minutes, and Cate springs up to grab our takeout from the delivery driver.

You're here to work. To help her create a few visuals for her reports. Not to undress her with her eyes, you freak! Get it together.

I'm able to reel it in better after we eat, the fried eggrolls and steamed dumplings nourishing my self control as much as they do my stomach. "You mind if I mess around with these for a bit?" I ask her when our plates are clear and she's sticking the leftovers in the fridge.

"Sure, knock yourself out," she calls over a shoulder before disappearing down the hallway that leads to her and Mindy's bedrooms and the one bathroom they share.

I slide her computer into my lap and import her raw data to our company's data visualization software, then get to work. It's already well-organized, like I should expect anything less from Cate, and it only takes me a few minutes to create some charts.

When she comes back into the room, Cate leans against the armrest of the couch closest to me to peer over my shoulder. "What's that?" She has her chin tipped toward a line graph I made with a trendline that shows our social media follower growth by platform. I show her what I did, how I made it.

"You're kinda cute when you get all nerdy," she says with the type of nonchalance I could only dream about, then curls her legs underneath her on the couch beside me. I dip my head to hide the way the tips of my ears turn red. The scent of peonies wafts into my nose when she leans closer, trailing one finger along another chart—this one a bar graph mapping days we've posted against our total sales for the day. When you look at some of our most recent posts, there's been a small uptick in sales right after.

I've made a lot of tables and charts in my life, but this one may be the most satisfying of them all.

"This is incredible," she whispers when I'm done, beaming at the bright laptop screen. "Can you do all my monthly reports from now on?"

I chuckle and shrug. "If you send me the data, I don't see why not."

Her mouth drops open and she smacks me lightly across the top of my tricep. "I was kidding! Cate Seymour doesn't take handouts."

Aside from a few light touches here and there—a squeeze of a shoulder after a particularly good take while filming something, a small caress to the back when we're moving in a confined space together—we haven't kissed since the first time about a week ago, after her last playoff game. It's been torture, and I think I've had enough of the punishment.

Trying to mirror her confidence, I catch her hand in mine, threading our fingers together on top of my knee. My chest warms when she lets me. "Fine, then maybe I can teach you how to do this on your own instead."

"Deal," she says, giving my hand a squeeze, and looks back at the computer. "Darius is going to be beside himself on Monday."

"Everyone's going to be impressed. This is impressive." *You're impressive.*

She nudges my ribs with her elbow. "Bet no one will suggest cutting any of my campaigns this time."

Wincing, I close my eyes and hang my head back on my shoulders. When I reopen them, it's to look at her. "I never apologized for that," I say in a small voice. Every so often, whether Cate and I are together or apart, I flash back to that day and cringe. Physically flinch, like I've been struck.

I'd panicked, and I let it cloud my judgment. Let it convince me I was doing the right thing, that she was the one overreacting with her death glares. "I didn't get it at the time, why it wasn't appropriate. I didn't let myself see why it would bother you."

"But you do now? See it?"

I dip my chin until I'm eye level with her. "I should've spoken with you in private. Doing that in front of the team, it came out wrong. Like I—"

"Like you're a giant know-it-all with a superiority complex?" she says sweetly, batting her eyelashes my way.

I gently flick her nose, resisting the desire to kiss the small hurt after. "I'm sorry. I should've asked you about them. Not told you what to do."

"In front of my boss," she adds. "And the world."

"Would it help if I got on my knees and groveled?"

"It might." Her lips are twisted to one side, like she's trying not to look too self-satisfied right now. It makes my heart thrum in my chest.

Without missing a beat, I slide from the couch to the floor, knees pressed into the soft shaggy carpet beneath me. Even with Cate still on the couch, we're nearly eye level. I take her hands in mine, clasping them together on her thighs, and try to muster up the most sincere puppy dog pout I can. I'm digging deep here—round eyes, soft mouth, relaxed jaw—the full nine yards. Because she deserves no less and both of us know it.

She sucks in a sharp inhale through her mouth and I swear I see her pulse jump in her throat when my lips part. "Cate I-wish-I-knew-your-middle-name-right-now Seymour."

She laughs and it sounds a little shaky. "It's Anne."

I nod. "Cate Anne Seymour. Please accept my sincerest apologies for behaving so childishly in the staff meeting. I was out of line, and for that I am truly, deeply sorry." It's hard to keep a straight face, requiring all the concentration I have, but somehow I manage.

Cate on the other hand seems torn between a fit of laughter and what I assume are tears of embarrassment. Her lips are rolled so tightly between her teeth, I'm surprised it doesn't hurt. When she finally speaks, in true Cate fashion, it's to whisper, "You forgot the part about how you were wrong and I was right, as always."

A growling sound rumbles from the back of my throat and there's no holding it back anymore. I pounce forward, gently tackling her to the back of the couch. An instant later, my lips meet hers, and while any normal person would taste like garlic for three days straight after the amount of Chinese food we consumed, she tastes like a strawberry mojito. A little bit of mint from her toothpaste—what she must've done when she slinked off to the bathroom, I realize—and a little bit of sweetness from her Chapstick. It's my new favorite drink.

With one arm cradling her spine and the other tangled in her hair, I pull her under me until she's lying flat with her head propped against the sofa's armrest. When her thighs part and our hips meet, she gasps, and my tongue sweeps between her lips.

This kiss feels different than the first we shared. That time was like a bridge being built, a new connection firing to life between us. It was exploring, but tentative.

This kiss is hungry. It's consuming. I've never kissed anyone like this before, never been kissed like this before. Not that I've gone on many dates or had many serious relationships over the years. Any serious relationships, if I'm honest. There was only Kira, back in college, and I think that was born more out of convenience than love. We shared six classes spread across two semesters. It made sense to team up, share notes. The connection may have turned physical, but that was as deep as it ever went. Skin level.

With Cate, it's like I'm trying to kiss past every layer of her. With each sweep of my tongue, each nibble of her lips, each roll of my hips, I can break down another wall, claw my way past her hard candy exterior and get to the gooey, melty center I crave.

I know she feels how much I want her, my hard length pressed against the inside of her left thigh. When she lets out a low groan, I slide a hand up her calf, trailing my fingertips up, up, up until they find the front of her leggings.

"Paul," she rasps, voice low and thick with desire. It makes my eyes roll into the back of my head, hearing her say my name like that. I add a little pressure, sweeping my first two fingers in a teasing circle at her center.

She tilts her head back and moans, one of her hands fisting the couch beneath her while the other tugs clumsily on the hem of my maroon T-shirt, wrinkling the faded Redwoods National Park logo on its front. I'm torn between touching her and helping her yank it off. My insatiable need to do anything for her, support her in any way I can, eventually wins out, and I help her pull the shirt over my head and toss it to the floor.

The second I return to her, she reaches for the fly of my jeans, doing her best to unbutton them blindly. This time, I gently still her fingers, using one hand to instead pin her wrists above her head. Her eagerness is driving me insane, in the best way possible, but my desire to stretch this moment, enjoy it for as long as I possibly can, is too strong to deny.

When Cate opens her mouth to protest, I silence her with a kiss, first to her lips and then, when she melts into my touch, I move to her jaw. I press a trail of kisses down to the hollow of her throat, where that alluring scent of peonies is strongest. It calls to me like a beacon.

In my distraction, I loosen my grip on Cate's wrists, and she runs her hands along my shoulders and down my back, leaving a trail of goosebumps in their wake. I feel like the jalapeño margarita she made for me. On fire, fizzing like a bottle of champagne under pressure, one second away from exploding.

Kissing over to her ear, I whisper, "Should we move to your room?"

I'm not worried about being found—Cate assured me we'd have the house to ourselves for the night—but this couch is far too small for all the things I've dreamed about doing to her since we started this project.

She nods, already pushing against my bare chest to move me. I chuckle, a barely audible sound, and press one more kiss to her lips before obliging.

CHAPTER 17

Cate

I THINK MY BRAIN might be short circuiting. It feels like it's projecting a dream I had the other night into some sort of virtual reality universe. It looks like my bedroom, it feels like my bed, the incredible kisser that is Paul Andrews certainly feels like Paul Andrews. And yet, this must be a dream.

Because he feels better than any man has any right to feel. He feels like someone showing up at your doorstep, looking a little wary and disheveled, because they didn't hear from you and needed to know you're okay. He feels like a home I always wanted, but never could find.

I'm straddling his lap now, his back wedged against a mountain of pillows by the headboard so he's halfway reclined, running my hands down his bare torso while he teases my lips with his teeth. I should feel more in control, on top like this, but I've never felt so out of it before in my life. It should scare me, this floating feeling, like the current of a lazy river lulling me around a blind bend, a waterfall waiting on the other side. It doesn't. It only makes me want to swim deeper. To let it take me out to sea.

Paul sucks in a sharp inhale that whistles through his teeth when I hook my fingertips into the waistband of his jeans. His eyes roll back for a moment and there's a dull thud when his head meets the headboard. I reach for his zipper for the second time tonight, and he stalls me with his hand. Again.

He at least has the decency to look pained when he meets my fiery gaze. "Are you sure?"

Am I sure? I haven't felt certain about much in weeks. Almost everything I thought I knew about Paul turned out to be wrong. It made me question things. *He* made me question things. Things I thought I knew about him. About myself.

In spite of it, or because of it, yes. My answer is yes. Because I've never felt more sure about anything in my entire life than I do right now, with the heat from Paul's palm setting my skin on fire and the burn from his kisses swelling my lips.

He mistakes my pause for doubt and the corners of his mouth turn down. "We don't have to…" His voice breaks at the end, and I rip my hand out of his to place it gently against the side of his face instead.

Cradling his sharp cheekbone, I lean in until our lips brush with every syllable. "I want this. I want *you*."

He hums, the sound coming from the base of his throat, and it pulses through me. It's like the warning before a dam releases its hold.

Impossibly fast, he sits up and rips my cropped T-shirt over my head in one motion, tossing it behind me. It hits a bookcase in the corner, toppling an old paperback copy of a Jen DeLuca book to the ground. I laugh and he swallows it with a kiss.

A second later and my bralette is on the floor with that old book and Paul is cradling the back of my neck while he flips us over so he's on top. I'd always thought of him as wiry and thin, but those long-sleeved shirts, buttoned snugly at the wrists, were hiding sinewy strength. Taut lines of muscle that flash and stretch when he moves. I want to kiss each and every curve.

Working together, we manage to slide my leggings off first with minimal difficulty. He's clumsier with his pants, wriggling out of them like a man on a mission. And judging by the heat in his navy blue eyes, he is one. I smile into another one of his kisses.

His lips leave mine, and I open my mouth to protest until they find a soft spot in the center of my collarbone. I arch my back, encouraging him further. Lower. He kisses another spot over to the right, just beneath my breast, and I breathe a sigh of pleasure.

He continues like that, kissing down to a spot right above my left hip bone, another on the outer edge of my right thigh. He takes a little extra time there and I open my eyes, wondering why, when he could be five inches to the left, exactly where I want him. I swear I hear him breathe the words, "You are a force, crazy girl," against my skin.

When I look down to see him kissing over to a spot on the inside of my knee, my stomach flips in understanding. He's kissing my bruises. Some of them barely even a mark anymore after weeks of healing, others stark purple against my gradually paling skin—the only part of fall I dislike.

My throat feels like I swallowed a baseball.

The sensation doesn't have time to last, though, because then Paul's fingers are sliding my underwear down my legs and his mouth is between my thighs. I lose my ability to hear, see, smell, taste, to feel anything other than the sweep and curl of his tongue as he finds a rhythm. Until my spine is completely arched off the bed and my fingers are fisted tightly in his sandy blond hair. Then I feel *everything,* all at once, and it's almost my undoing.

"Paul," I gasp and he groans at the sound of his name, quickening his pace. My thighs feel like Jello, a sensation I'm familiar with from my occasional self-care sessions. I'm close. Too close.

I give his hair a less-than-gentle tug and he finally pauses to look up. He's wearing a lazy smile, those navy eyes heavy and glazed, and he's so beautiful I think my heart might jump right out of my chest.

How did I not notice it before? How could I have missed it?

I knew Paul Andrews was objectively attractive, but that was nothing compared to the way I see him now. The man I know now. The one who smiles at me like he just woke up from the best nap of his life while on vacation at a five-star beach resort in some fancy destination you have to take at least two planes to get to.

"Now" is what I say to him, lifting my brows impatiently, and he springs to life once more.

There's a rustling noise followed by the muffled sound of foil tearing and then he's back on top of me. He cradles each of my thighs in his hands, spreading me wider, and brushes against my entrance. My eyes roll back in my head at the first feel of him, like even that small amount of contact might be too much.

I have to try, though. Try for more. I twine my fingers behind his back and urge him closer. When he finally sinks into me, it's like all the planets in the galaxy aligning. A perfect day when your favorite latte is made just right, when your email inbox is at zero and no one's bothering you, when you're alone in the world with the person you—

I wrap my legs around his hips as Paul increases his speed. In the darkness, his lips find mine again, and the sound he makes when they do sends me spiraling over the edge. When I tighten my grip on his waist, lips parted in a breathless moan, he follows me down.

CHAPTER 18

Cate

IT'S NOT THE FIRST time I've pictured myself tackling Paul Andrews to the ground in the middle of an all-hands meeting. However, it is the first time I've imagined him shirtless, the firm planes of his chest now etched into my memory like smooth glass struck by the sharp edge of a stone. So perfect it should hang in the Sistine Chapel, soft rays of sunlight illuminating every hidden freckle.

I can practically feel how hot his skin would be beneath my touch, the way he'd shiver when I stroke my fingertips through the soft tuft of hair above the waistband of his slacks.

The sound of Paul clearing his throat—while his boss, now back from vacation, drones on in the background about submitting receipts for reimbursement—evaporates the fantasy, and I catch him blinking his big, navy eyes at me. One corner of his mouth is drawn up, like he knows exactly what I was thinking about. *Caught*.

I slide my eyes to his hands pressed too firmly against the surface of the conference room table, and my smirk mirrors his. *At least I'm not the only one daydreaming.*

We crossed a line the other night. We're coworkers. Coworkers don't casually hook up with one another. Or maybe they do, but certainly not coworkers like Paul and me. We're conscientious. We're professional. But we saw that line, drawn between us in thick, black Sharpie marker with a big red sign reading "STOP!" beside it, and we sprinted right on past it.

Keeping the kiss a secret had been hard enough. Lord knows Mindy's already hot on my trail, sniffing around every time she comes back from her boyfriend's house or her parents' house, like she knows Paul was there. Like she might find him hiding in my bedroom closet still. I won't be able to keep it from her much longer, but she's not just my roommate or just my best friend. She's also a colleague, and I'm not ready for work to find out about Paul and me. I'm not ready to jinx whatever it is we have all because we went blabbing about it and then word spread like a wildfire and now we have to fill out some sort of love contract with Jerry in Human Resources.

Love. Geez, Cate. Pump the brakes.

Why does that stupid little word keep trying to wiggle its way into my brain and out of my mouth?

A month ago, I hated this guy. Well, I came as close to hating him as I've ever hated anybody, at least. We're not *in love*.

So why does my stomach flutter every time he enters the room? I used to run in the opposite direction when I saw him coming. Now I can't. Stop. Thinking. About. Him. Even when I absolutely, most definitely should. Like in this staff meeting where I'm practically drooling onto the glass tabletop under my fists, balled to keep them in check.

If I wasn't already sure that something had gone severely wrong with my brain since I started spending time with Paul Andrews, now there is no mistaking it. While Darius shares an update on the displays we'll be putting into dozens of Whole Foods across the country for the CitraCrush launch—something I care *deeply* about—I hold Paul's gaze instead of listening. And run my tongue along my upper lip, painfully slowly, delighting in the way he writhes in his chair, unable to take his eyes off me.

"Cate, looks like you're up next on the agenda," Darius says and I jump, a kid caught passing notes in class. When I turn to him, he's smiling, patient. Unsuspecting, I think (read: hope).

I release a breath and nod, pulling up the data visualizations Paul helped me with over lunch yesterday. His reports on Operation: New Soda Launch—Paul's name for it, not mine—had gone over so well with Darius last week that Paul insisted on helping me again, this time with a completely separate project. I'd tried to stop him. Or at least, I offered to do it myself, now that he'd (kind of) taught me how. He's already doing more than enough, between helping me film and edit. I'm not sure when the man sleeps.

Unless he's with me.

It's been almost two weeks since our first time, and since then he's stayed at my place three nights. Only when Mindy's gone, of course. It hasn't been enough, not nearly enough. I've never wanted my best friend out of the house so much in my life. And then I feel guilty for sneaking around behind her back in the first place, which sends me into a mini downward spiral that can only be cured by more alone time with Paul.

I can't help it, though. Every time he looks at me with that closed-lip, lopsided smile, I want to climb him like a tree. Or a bean-pole. *Shut up, Cate. You can't afford to start giggling like a schoolgirl right now.*

I'd practically jumped him the other day, right here in the conference room, while we were working on the very reports I'm presenting now. In the span of an hour, he'd not only revamped my sad Excel sheets using a software I couldn't even pronounce, but he'd also found a way for me to save almost a thousand dollars a month. It might have annoyed me once, him messing around with my life's work. But this didn't feel like a critique and he didn't feel like a judge. We were partners. "I'm only offering suggestions. You know what's best," he'd told me when he spun the laptop around to show me what he'd discovered.

And damn if he isn't sexy as hell when he talks data to me.

Ultimately, I decided to take Paul's advice. That's the update I'm sharing with the team now as Darius nods and grins at me like *he's* just taught me to ride a bike and now proudly watches me pedal down the road without my training wheels for the first time. All the while, Paul smiles that lopsided half-smile and silently nods his encouragement in my direction. He'd never take the credit, even though he should. He'd much rather sit back and let me shine, content that he helped me do it. My chest squeezes.

In the weeks we've been sneaking around, neither of us has dared to ask where it's heading. What we are to each other. It's as if we both entered into a silent pact not to question it, not to ruin it. Not yet.

"Great work, Cate," Darius says when I've finished. "Looking forward to seeing your plans for reinvesting that extra cash." With a passing wink in my direction, he turns back to the agenda and concludes the meeting.

When I look at Paul again, I can tell from the heat in his eyes that he's thinking about the way I thanked him for his help with this. A red-hot flush creeps up the back of my neck and I move my cursor back and forth on my computer's trackpad for something to distract me while the room slowly empties out.

"Okay, what's the deal with you and Andrews?" Mindy whispers when we get back to our desks.

I freeze, shoulders stiff as a board, hand hovering over my mouse. "What do you mean?" The words come out more robotic than I intend, betraying my fear.

I hear the sound of creaky plastic wheels rolling against old carpet and feel her peering over my shoulder. "I mean the two of you making eyes at each other the entire staff meeting. I've seen you stare at him before, but in more of an *I'm pretending to shoot torpedoes at you* way. This was different. Still intense, but different."

Crap. "We weren't making eyes." I should turn around and face Mindy, reassure her that she's mistaken, but I'm afraid of what she might see on my face. She's clearly more observant than I gave her credit for. "He helped me with those reports. I probably looked at him to make sure I was sharing the information correctly. That's all."

"Oh really?" She swivels around the side of my desk until it's too awkward for me *not* to look at her. I do, resisting the urge to wince. "Because it looked like maybe he's been helping you with more than your reports." Pausing for dramatic effect, she taps a green-painted fingertip against her bottom lip. "Or is it the other way around?"

"Mindy!" I hiss, widening my eyes meaningfully then looking around our cubicle to make sure no one else heard.

"I knew it! You've been hooking up, haven't you?"

"MINDY!" I say again, louder this time. I thank my lucky stars it's lunchtime and most of the desks around us are empty.

She holds up her hands defensively. "Hey, I'm not judging. But I must ask that you two don't defile our sofa. I eat there." She wrinkles her nose and shakes her shoulders in a mock shiver.

I want to melt into the floor. No, I want to melt through the floor and into the ground beneath this godforsaken building.

I muster up the best glare I can, aimed squarely at Mindy, but even I can tell it lacks zeal. "We aren't going to do it on the couch," I hedge, and her face lights up with victory while mine falls a little further.

In my heart of hearts, I knew I wouldn't be able to hide this from her forever. I mean, we live together, for crying out loud. I did (stupidly) believe I'd have more time.

More time to exist in our little bubble before we need to broach the tough subjects.

More time to figure out how to deal with the fact that we work at the same company, and eventually our relationship could be considered a liability. VitaPop's handbook is pretty sparse, part of the startup culture fostered here by its founders, and I'm ninety percent sure it doesn't have any rules against getting cozy with coworkers, but I've been too afraid to actually check it.

We don't even have an HR department. We have Jerry, our Employee Engagement Partner. He calls himself the Director of Fun and basically does team building. Jerry will understand, right? We're just having a little fun, nothing wrong with that!

The bigger question is: will Darius understand?

If I were the type of person to point fingers, which I am, it's his fault we're in this mess to begin with. Thinking back to that meeting with the three of us, the one that started it all, I remember how angry and disappointed I'd been. My own boss, bringing in an outsider because he didn't think I could do this on my own.

Then I think about the past few weeks with Paul. His idea to do the campaign ourselves, his willingness to try almost anything. The man didn't even get upset when I flooded his desk with soda.

More than that, I think about the way he pushed himself into my house when I got hurt. I think about the look of concern in his eyes when he handed me a glass of water. When he asked me why. Why I do what I do. At the time, there's no way he could've known it was a loaded question, but something about the way he listened so intently to my answer gave me the impression he understood more than he let on.

I don't have to hide my sharp and prickly edges from him. Sometimes I lay it on thick, find new ways to push his buttons, to see how he'll react. I swear his eyes shine a little brighter when I do, lit by the challenge. Like he enjoys me best that way, when I don't hold back.

It's freeing, not having to hide what I'm thinking. Not having to try to be anything other than me. I'm not sure it's ever been this easy with anyone, not even with Mindy, in the beginning. I find myself willing to do almost anything—to corrupt my morals, to sneak around—not to lose what Paul and I have.

Mindy arches an eyebrow at me and crosses her arms over her chest.

"Okay, fine," I whine, letting my head loll back on my neck. "Things have gotten a little friendly between us." With pleading eyes, I return my gaze to hers. "Please don't tell anyone."

"Why, because you're scared of the big bosses finding out or because you're hooking up with your archnemesis and word getting out could kill your personal brand?"

For the first time since we started this interrogation, my lips twitch toward a smile. "Both?"

She rolls her eyes, but there's no malice in it. "As I said before, I'm not judging. Have a little fun, get to know him, do whatever you gotta do." Then she pins me with a stare I like to call the "Mindy special." "Remember, eyes on the prize. Nominations for the Edie Awards are due in a couple weeks. Right after the product launch."

Right. The award that started me down this road in the first place.

I haven't told Paul about it. Not even that night, when we saw the numbers on his screen and realized: Holy shit, we're actually pretty good at this. Partially because he hadn't asked and mostly because I felt like it might, I don't know, cheapen it. What we're doing together. Would he think I'm using him? Am I using him? Sometimes I can be so narrow-minded it's hard to tell.

That's not what this feels like, though. It feels like someone new finally saw me. Not just the surface, the things I let everyone see, but all the dark and messy layers underneath.

Paul saw the mushy center in my hard-candied shell and ran toward it instead of away. Now, there's so much more between us than a project or the chance to win a stupid marketing award. Maybe too much.

Swallowing the dryness in the back of my mouth, I force a smile, one I hope is reassuring. "Don't worry about me, Min. I've got this."

I don't think she heard the quiver in my voice.

CHAPTER 19

Paul

"THAT LOOKS HORRENDOUS," I say bluntly, squaring my shoulders with the countertop like I'm about to do battle. It feels like I am, but not with the faux marble that's actually made from cheap, oddly durable, laminate. It's with what's on top of it that I have a bone to pick.

"It can't be any worse than the margarita that, I admit, was mostly jalapeño seeds," Cate shoots back, leaning closer to the fizzy cup of death. She takes a quick sniff and her face goes still, like she's trying hard to keep it neutral.

I throw my hands out, palms exposed at the concoction that is, quite possibly, the most unappealing brown color I've ever come into contact with. "Then why don't you taste this one?"

At this, she turns a grin on me that's got more fake sweetener in it than the beverage in question. "The audience wants you." She bats her lashes at me, pale blonde strands so long they caress her cheeks on every blink, and a hunger rears up in me that I simply do not have time for right now. "Their Soda King," she adds, voice cracking on the last word. A desperate attempt to hold her laughter in.

She's referring to my most recent online nickname. The comments have only escalated in recent weeks, and one fan even started making what Cate calls "thirst trap edits" of me using some of the footage we've posted. I begged Bethany to keep her thoughts and the video links to herself, but I'm expecting another call from my dad any day now, likely more frantic than the last.

"Come on, it doesn't even smell that bad. They said it tastes like bubble gum," she says, tone cajoling once more.

"They" are the same TikTok users commenting things like "The soda pie isn't the only thing that just exploded" and "it" is the cup full of ice, VitaPop Root Beer, and sugar free lemonade currently condensing before us. Clearly none of these things can be trusted, and Cate is on a fast-track to joining that list.

With one final withering look in her direction, I nod for her to start filming. The squeak of glee she makes, followed by a quick clap of her hands, makes my stomach roll, and not in a good way.

It takes everything in me to keep from spewing out the liquid after my first deep sip through the jumbo pink straw Cate selected specifically for this video. In fact, the only thing that makes me swallow is the fear of what my "fans" might comment if she posts a clip of me spitting it up.

After the camera is turned off and I've rinsed my mouth out with my travel-size Listerine bottle—*twice*—I slide one leg onto a barstool at the edge of the counter, keeping the foot of the other planted on the tile floor. A battle stance. "Before you head to practice, I wanted to show you something." My voice is low, a secret whispered in an alley, and I clear my throat in an attempt to act more natural.

Cate slings her lavender fabric backpack over a shoulder and pads over, head angled at my now open laptop. The scent of peonies floods my nose when her chest brushes the back of my shoulder, light as a butterfly's wings. If she notices my nerves, she doesn't say anything. My hand trembles as it pushes play on the video I stayed up way too late working on last night.

I keep my eyes trained on the screen without seeing much of anything. I've already watched it more than a hundred times, anyway. It took forever to get the stop-motion effect right, to get the sodas placed and lined up and synced with the music just so.

When I hear Cate snort during one part, some of my anxiety evaporates, and a smile tugs at my lips.

"I'm not sure what we'd use it for," I say when it ends, overly conscious of my reflection in the dark computer screen. "It was just an idea I had."

"I love it," she says easily, and my chest deflates on a large exhale of air and puffs with pride at the same time. Only Cate would make me defy the laws of physics. Or biology. Chemistry?

Shut up, Paul.

"It would be great on a display. Something flashy, like the end of an aisle at a big chain store," she's saying, and I make a half-turn on my stool to look up at her. "You should show this to Darius before he leaves today. The contract with Whole Foods isn't finalized yet, he might be able to negotiate one in."

Looking off into the middle distance, I bite the inside of my cheek. Pitch this to Darius, myself? It feels like crossing some invisible line. It's one thing if I'm helping Cate. Doing what she tells me and giving her most of the credit. It's another thing entirely for me to produce my own project. The fact Cate's even suggested it tells me two things.

One: She no longer sees us as rivals. For this, I am ecstatic. I could do jumping jacks and cartwheels through the test kitchen right now.

Two: She still doesn't know why I know all these video editing programs like the back of my hand, or that my dad called me concerned the first time he saw me in one of our videos. Not that I'd ever, *ever*, admit the latter to her, but that's beside the point.

The bottom line is, she doesn't really know me.

My nostrils flare at the realization, and all my enthusiasm drains away.

"Oh, I wouldn't want to bother him with this," I hedge, avoiding her prying eyes. I can feel them probing my face, her eyebrows practically forming a giant question mark in the center of her forehead. I quickly slam my laptop shut, jumping at the sound of plastic hitting plastic. "We probably don't have the budget to add on something like that, and it's not that good anyway."

"Paul." She emphasizes my name, and I stop trying to slide my computer into my bag. Covertly, she glances over each of her shoulders to ensure we're alone, then gently grabs my chin between her index finger and thumb, forcing me to look at her. "It *is* good. It could be a freaking commercial."

For a few moments, she stares deeply into my eyes, and I notice how bright the flecks of gold in hers shine, reflecting the light streaming in from the windows beside her. She lets go of my chin and it feels like I've lost a limb.

Her mouth twists to one side and... *Oh no.* I know that look. After a deep breath she says, "If you don't want to tell me, I get it. I mean, I don't really, because you haven't told me. Maybe it's personal, maybe you're embarrassed." She blinks at something over my shoulder, a frown pulling her lips down. "Maybe we aren't that close."

I open my mouth to object, not knowing at all what's going to come out, only that I vehemently disagree. If anything, it's the opposite. We are close. I want to be *closer* to her. I've been kicking myself for not telling her this sooner, before we slept together. At the same time, I've had no clue how to bring it up, how to talk about it.

Luckily, or unluckily, she cuts me off with a wave of her hand. "You don't make videos like this because you took one class a billion years ago or whatever line you fed me."

And there it is. I swallow, waiting for the final blow.

Cate dips her head until we're inches apart, her hazel eyes boring into me like the summer sun at high noon. "If you don't want to tell me, that's okay. But I'm going to ask one more time: How do you know how to do this and, more importantly, why are you so hell-bent on keeping it a secret?"

I drop her gaze, looking instead at a freckle on her knee. She's wearing the brown corduroy skirt today, my favorite. I resist the urge to reach out and run my fingertips along its bottom hem, to connect her freckles like a constellation.

Instead, I tilt my head back to look at her fully. And then I tell her everything.

I got my first camcorder when I was thirteen. I had begged and begged my parents for it for a full year and they'd told me time and again that a boy my age had no use for such a thing. "Go kick a ball around," my dad would say good-naturedly. "Spend time outside."

But it was for that exact reason I wanted the camera. We lived on the outskirts of Eugene, Oregon, in a small community encased by towering evergreens that hazed over with gray on cool winter mornings and radiated the most vibrant colors of the rainbow on fall afternoons. From the moment I was old enough to explore the trails and lakes that bordered my home alone, I was obsessed.

And the only thing I was more obsessed with than communing with nature itself were the wildlife shows my dad would put on TV for his afternoon naps. It wasn't enough to merely watch *Jack Hanna's Into the Wild*, I wanted to be him. Except maybe without some of the wild animal bits. I don't think I'd enjoy possibly getting mauled.

After two years of being told "no," there it was. The last box I unwrapped on my thirteenth birthday. I blew through the tape that came with it in two days and used every penny of my allowance to buy more. My best friend Jake joined me on my adventures through the wilderness, each of us taking turns talking to the camera about where we were, what we found. We named every tree and plant and bird call that we could, which at the time wasn't very many, though that would shortly change.

Eventually the camcorder was replaced by more advanced smartphones, and Jake and I started sharing our footage on a shared YouTube channel. Bad, grainy shots got axed or cleaned up in Adobe's After Effects program, another big dent to my savings account—which by this point came from an after school job at our local pizza shop instead of my parents.

We got older and our skills improved. Jake could riff unscripted on the camera perfectly, like he belonged there. He did, had that type of star power you can't define with words but know when you see it. Bright eyes, a wide smile. Not a self-conscious bone in his body.

My shots got better and better, until there was less and less to clean up in post. We got our driver's licenses and were no longer sequestered to the woods that rimmed our homes or the state parks we could convince our parents to drive us to.

That's where it came from, the idea that will forever haunt me.

Our subscriber count on YouTube had ballooned to over 100K by the time we started our senior year of high school, and though most of our friends had found other interests to captivate their attention—girls and sports and college applications—Jake and I were single-minded. This was our future, this was what we'd do with our lives. Him on camera and me behind it, visiting the most stunning places the world has to offer.

The day I told my parents I planned to take a gap year after high school to backpack across Europe was the second scariest day of my life. The first would come eight months later. I thought my dad's head would implode, right then and there. The color red his face had flushed was unnatural, somewhere between a plum and an overripe tomato.

"This little video thing. I know you're having fun," he'd said, fist clenching and unclenching around his glass of iced tea so hard I thought it might break. "But it needs to stop. It's high time you get serious about your future. Your math scores are stellar. You could follow in my footsteps, start a career in wealth management with a degree from the right university." I'd fought myself not to roll my eyes and won, thankfully, but made a mental note to bomb my next AP Statistics test out of spite.

My mom was better at restraining herself, gently talking me through the potential repercussions—how it may be harder to pick school back up after so much time off, how it might delay any potential career I wanted—but ultimately she told me the decision was mine.

She found some way to convince my dad to back off too, using a type of magic only acquired after twenty-five years of marriage.

About a month after graduation, Jake and I flew to Seville and started our journey. Sometimes we were outside for more than fourteen hours a day, spending our nights in cheap hostels that barely had running water, in rooms packed full of people from all over the world. Other times we camped, not wanting to break our treks to head back to the nearest city. Despite the conditions, despite sometimes not knowing where we'd get our next hot meal or where we'd lay our heads at night, each day was better than the one before.

The hiking trails grew gradually more dangerous the further we went. From Spain, we moved north to France, with our final stops planned in Germany. Lake Schrecksee would be the culmination of months of hard work: blood, sweat, and painful deliberation over which clips to delete when the storage on our devices became full.

Tucked away in the Bavarian Alps near the border to Austria, the lake itself is located a mile above sea level. When we crested the summit of the final peak on a balmy day in late September, the water looked like a piece of sea glass surrounded on all sides by fuzzy moss. The view was breathtaking, even more than the steep three-hour climb to reach it.

Jake and I spent hours up there. We got the footage we wanted early on, climbing one final peak to the last viewpoint of the lake before trekking back down to a partially flat expanse where we could take a hard-earned break. Munching on protein bars and trail mix we'd stuffed into our backpacks, the conversation naturally drifted to what came next.

This was our last stop. According to the plan, we'd work our way to Munich and all that was left to do was board a plane for home. Neither of us was quite ready to see it end, but funds were running low and we were fast approaching the deadline to apply to colleges for next year, if that's what we wanted.

After a stretch of contemplative silence, my eyes hung on the rapidly-dimming sky. With a lopsided smile, I told Jake if we left right then, we might have time to find a cheap hotel and take our first hot showers in what might have been weeks.

"Let's stay a little longer," he pressed, sweeping a hand across our view. Despite how long the shadows from the trees behind us were growing, it was hard to resist the snare of its beauty.

"One more week," Jake begged, jabbing me in the ribs with his pointy elbow, earning a surprised look from me. He had it all planned out, he said. We'd still head toward Munich, but hit Lake Tegernsee first for a few days, then treat ourselves to a stay in a real hotel for our final nights with the last of our money before flying back to America.

His enthusiasm was contagious, a siren's song, luring me away from the plan against my better judgment. Jake could be relentless when he wanted something, and this time was no different. By the time we'd come to an agreement, over four hours had passed since we'd stopped to rest and the sun was quickly descending toward the distant horizon.

The trail we'd taken isn't known for being dangerous, but at the time, some of the pathways were slick from a heavy rainfall a few days earlier, while others were barely paths at all. Being unfamiliar with the route, we'd need to take our time descending. I looked at the path of the sun and a tremor rattled through my gut.

"If we move quickly, we can get to the second set of trailheads before dusk," I said, cutting off the conversation about Munich. Jake followed my line of sight, noting the dwindling light in the sky, then nodded solemnly. My muscles relaxed—I'd been expecting another argument.

We wouldn't have to worry about getting lost, but there were no places to stop along the way. Our flashlight beams wouldn't be much help over the stony terrain. We *had* to make it to the easier, lower section of the hike before complete darkness set in, and that meant descending a lot faster than we'd climbed.

I'd been hiking too quickly to see exactly how it happened and what caused Jake to trip. I'd been too focused, trying to outrun the prickle on the back of my neck.

Only one of us walked off the mountain that evening.

I don't have much practice sharing it, no rehearsed script. I stopped telling people about Jake my first year of college. Back then, I'd lead with the worst news first: My best friend, he died on a hiking trip. I watched him fall, unable to stop it.

As soon as the words would leave my lips, it was like a chemical reaction. It happened the same way every time. First, their forehead would crease. Then, they'd fold their arms around themselves, a barrier that could protect them from this information. Their frown would be a perfect upside-down curve, bottom lip jutting out a tiny bit farther than the top.

Jake's passing was the reason I stopped making videos. Why I went to college for finance and took this accounting job when VitaPop was too small to afford anything better than a recent graduate.

But that look of pity, of what might be judgment lurking beneath the surface, that's why I stopped telling people about it.

Without wanting to, I search Cate's face for it now.

She's taken a seat on the stool beside mine, one forearm pressed against the cool tabletop, hands folded near its edge. Her jaw is soft, lips touching but not tightly.

I search and search but don't see pity there. Sorrow, yes, mixed with something else. She dips her chin, the movement almost too shallow to notice, and then I'm sure. It's understanding.

When I finish, she places a hand on top of mine, stilling the tremor in my fingers. "I'm sorry that happened to Jake, and to you. I'm severely unqualified to offer advice on this subject, so I won't. I can't tell you I know exactly how you're feeling, because I'm sure I don't. But I am going to say something a little candid and a lot important, and I need you to hear it." She bobs her head, searching for my gaze while I resist giving it to her.

Ultimately, she wins, like she usually does. Her voice is quiet, but even, when she tells me, "What happened to your friend is tragic, and it's okay to grieve his loss, but it was not your fault. You can't blame yourself." She says the words with her whole body and I swear I can feel them against my skin.

"You can try to live your whole life based on what others think is the better path, what they want from you. And you may even be content there from time to time. But it will not make that part of you, or the grief you feel, go away. You're doing yourself a disservice by believing it will."

I swallow. In my story, I shared the facts. Who Jake was to me, what we were to each other. What happened on the top of that mountain, and briefly afterward. And still, she saw right through me.

I nod, and she gives my hand a small squeeze. "I know," I say, because it's what I'm supposed to say, but I'm still not sure I believe it.

CHAPTER 20

Paul

CATE HAS A SCRIMMAGE today. I didn't want to ask her what that meant when she told me, why it was different than a regular game. It felt like something I should already know. Sure, we had stopped playing head games with one another, like *Who Has the Upper Hand Now*, out of spite. We only played for fun now, and only occasionally. But still, I didn't want to lose another round.

We met for coffee this morning before she had to go warm up. She'd picked the place, a tiny cafe in her neighborhood that doubles as a plant store. I recognized a few varieties from her desk at work and her living room. It must be her supplier. I'm not sure why that made me smile. Maybe it felt like she was peeling back another layer, inviting me into another sliver of her life.

As we sat across from one another at a small wooden table that rocked to and fro each time we moved, I'd only hesitated for a moment after she said the word. Still, she'd taken one look at me, the steam from the latte in her hand wafting in front of her face, and smirked. That tiny little twitch of her lips. It made me want to burn the whole coffee shop to the ground. It made me want to kiss her.

Instead, I set my jaw and blinked until she explained, *unprompted*, it meant the game didn't count. Then she oh-so-casually set her paper hot cup down, jostling the walnut table again, and cocked her head to the side innocently to add, "We already secured our spot in the championship."

In my head, I made an upside-down smile and shallowly nodded. *That's cool*, I'd said. *Good for you.*

In reality, I grinned like an idiot. I pumped my fist in the air between us, nearly knocking over both our drinks in the process. In reality, I cheered, "Yes!" like I'd witnessed their game-winning try myself. (Apparently, this is what they call a touchdown in rugby. Yes, I Googled it, sue me.)

Cate laughed. It was more like a giggle if you ask me, though she'd never agree to that. It made my leg shake, a straight hit of dopamine to every neuron in my brain. I've been jonesing for it again ever since.

I should be there now, at her scrimmage. This morning, with my nervous system already flooded with adrenaline, I nearly invited myself. My mouth was open, the words on the tip of my tongue. And then I lost my nerve.

It felt too close to the very thing we'd been dancing around and avoiding.

A different line to cross than the one we'd already jumped right over. The *define the relationship* line. In my twenty-eight years on this earth, I'd never had one of those conversations. I didn't have the wherewithal to start one now. In this game, I would be happy to let Cate take the lead.

Now as I sit here on the sagging loveseat in my empty apartment, laptop balanced on my thighs, staring at a half-written email to Darius in which I'm supposed to be sharing the stop-motion commercial I made, I realize how stupid that was.

Crossing a line. We've literally had sex. Several times. In the same night. *That* was crossing a line. And we hadn't just crossed it. Oh no. We'd barrelled straight over it, smashed it into the ground like freshly-poured cement under one of those machines with the giant rollers on the front. For weeks, since our first kiss at her house, I'd been dying for it. Aching for it. And it had been everything I'd imagined and then some.

And now I'm worried about going to watch her play at a goddamn scrimmage?

No, I'd been a chicken. I was afraid to ask her. Afraid she might turn me down and, although I'd still end up in the same place, I'd be a reject on top of it.

I pinch my nose between my thumb and forefinger and try to focus on the email I'm writing. Half-drafted was a stretch, I realize. All I have so far is:

`Hi Darius,`

`I hope this email finds you well.`

That's it. I groan and hit the backspace until the first and only full sentence is erased from existence. Has an email ever found anyone well? Certainly not me.

My phone buzzes on the coffee table and I grab for it like a lifeline, almost sending it skittering to the floor. Expecting a text, my eyebrows shoot up on my forehead when it keeps on buzzing. A phone call from an unsaved number.

Groaning, I mute it and set it back on the table. Telemarketer, probably. No matter how many you block, more will only find you.

After about a minute, it buzzes again, signaling a new voicemail. Odd. The spammers don't usually leave messages.

Curious, I play it on speakerphone. A cold sweat breaks out on my brow seconds later. I grip the phone so tightly in my hand I'm surprised the plastic brick doesn't snap in half from the force.

It's a voice I haven't heard in almost a decade. One that makes me want to flip the coffee table over, throw my phone at the wall, and weep at the same time.

She sounds older than I remember, her voice weathered but soft, like a well-loved T-shirt. She wants to know if I'll be coming home for the memorial. She tells me she'd love to see me, the whole family would.

What's left of it.

Jake's mom. My chest cracks open at her quiet plea. The resignation she tries to hide because she knows I won't be there. I can't. Even now, thinking about it, I feel like I'm back on that mountain. Men and women dressed in orange and black uniforms move around me, shouting in a language I can't understand, but I'm frozen. Rooted to the spot. The first time I became the statue.

My chest heaves with every rattled breath and I shake my head back and forth too many times. No. I can't. She'll understand. She has to understand.

The phone buzzes in my hand again, once this time. A text from an unsaved number.

It's probably her again. She's sensed my refusal and changed tactics. I go to clear the notification with the swipe of my thumb, but one word of the incoming message catches my eye first: Cate.

Tapping it brings up a new text thread, only one gray message bubble at the top. The letters jumble before my eyes until I can't make sense of the alphabet anymore.

"Thanks for coming," Mindy says with a stiff smile. Her hand is braced against the door to the house she shares with Cate. She keeps looking, not covertly at all, between me in the doorway and the dark hallway behind her. You'd think I'm a drug dealer by the way she keeps her chin ducked. I blink at her expectantly, hands twitching, my whole body urging me to push her aside and run inside the house if she takes one moment longer.

"I wasn't sure if I should..." She trails off, again searching for something over her shoulder. Then she straightens and meets my eyes for the first time. There's a determined set to her jaw that wasn't there before. "I don't think she should be alone and my parents will literally freak if I miss family dinner." It sounds like she's trying to convince herself.

"She doesn't know I'm here?" I venture, ducking my head closer to Mindy's to keep my voice low.

"She does now!" a dry voice calls from the living room, making Mindy and I jump.

I look squarely at Mindy and say, "You did the right thing." She nods, eyes softening with both relief and a little regret, and steps back to invite me in. It's a little strange, being formally asked to enter a house I've already been in half a dozen times. My cheeks heat at the memory of my last visit.

The warmth doesn't last long. My stomach hollows out when I first see Cate on the couch, Mindy trailing me into the living room like a dog that just threw up on the carpet. Cate isn't a tall girl, but she's never looked so small. Not even the last time I was here for this same reason, only that time I had no idea what I was walking into. It had caught me off guard, her standing there with those frozen veggies pressed to her head.

After that, I thought knowing would be better. Knowing she was hurt, knowing she needed my help.

It's not. Knowing is so much worse.

"Be kind, it's not his fault," Mindy says from over my shoulder, and Cate's nostrils flare when the two women make eye contact.

"Oh, don't worry," Cate says too sweetly. She tries to fold her arms over her chest, then winces and drops them back onto her blanket-covered lap. "In this case I fully plan on shooting the messenger." The threat has no bite to it and I hear Mindy snort as she disappears toward the front door.

Cate's eyes meet mine and she lifts an antagonistic brow. "Let me guess, you're on invalid duty again, doc?"

"I'm thinking about adding it as a new skill to my resume, actually." I slide onto the sofa beside her, picking up her feet to place them across my thighs. "Maybe turn this whole caregiver thing into a side hustle."

Though it physically pains her, and perhaps a little emotionally too, Cate chuckles. She sinks deeper into the throw pillow behind her and lets her head roll back, eyes slowly closing.

I can finally get a good look at her, and she looks...

She catches me frowning and lightly kicks my stomach. "Hey, there will be none of that."

I catch her foot in my hand and apply a small amount of pressure to her arch with my thumb. She groans, low and throaty, and I'm pretty sure the way it makes me feel is illegal in at least five countries.

"I take it back. You can do and say whatever you want, as long as you don't stop that."

Biting back a smile, I wrap both hands around her foot, fingertips kneading the sole. "If I'd known this was all it took to turn you into putty, I'd have done it a long time ago."

"I'm sure our coworkers would have been thrilled to witness that in the middle of the conference room," she muses, and I choke on my laugh.

With her eyes fully closed, I chance another glance at her. There's blue and purple bruising under her eye sockets and over the bridge of her nose. It's as though someone—very badly—traced the bottom outline of snorkeling goggles onto her face with a marker. I wish that's all it was.

More bruising peeks out of the loose collar of her T-shirt. I can't tell how far down it goes, only that it seems concentrated around her clavicles.

You shouldn't let her sleep, a niggling voice whispers to me, and my eyes snap open wide. *The doctor said she has a concussion.*

I pinch her big toe and she opens one eye. "Maybe you should sit up a little more," I hedge, and that one little eye rolls back at me.

"I'm fine, Dad. I was simply resting my eyes. Besides, that whole not sleeping with a concussion thing is a myth."

"Am I so easy to read?"

"You might as well have a neon sign flashing on your forehead." Her mouth twists into a smirk and I want to kiss it off her, but I know I shouldn't.

"You're doing it again," she warns, chin pointing in the direction of my mouth, which must be frowning. I pinch my lips together and try to make my face look more neutral. By Cate's answering half-smile, I probably only look constipated.

"So tell me what happened," I say, picking up her other foot to massage. "You took on a bear and the bear won, I presume?"

"Something like that," she answers with a shrug of one shoulder. "Except I still won, technically. I took the hit right before the try zone but my team was able to put it in goal on the next play. The hairline fracture to my nose was totally worth it."

I incline my head. "I know you're using words I've heard before, but I didn't comprehend any of that."

She sniffs a laugh and digs her heel into my leg. "You have to come to a game sometime. The terminology won't make sense until you see it in action."

It takes everything in me not to freeze at her casual tone, to keep gently kneading her foot and then her calf. My thoughts drift to my earlier dilemma, back when my biggest worry was an email to Darius—which I still haven't sent, now that I think about it—and being too pigheaded to invite myself to her scrimmage. I blow out a breath, feeling grateful for it now. To see her take a hit like this, up close and personal? I don't know what I would've done.

We both stay quiet, and I get the sense that I was supposed to say something, but I've already forgotten what it was and too much time has passed to revisit it. Cate's leg stiffens and I relax my grip on her bare foot, hoping I haven't hurt her.

I stare at the TV, the same British show playing in the background as the first time I came here. In it, they're trekking through a dense forest, leaves crunching underfoot. It reminds me of our afternoon at the orchard, a thin blanket of red and orange and yellow littering the ground near the barn, dropped by the ancient Rocky Mountain maple trees dotting the property.

Before the words are fully formed, I say, "I'm sorry you won't get to play in the championship game. If you want, I can sit on the bench with you. We can scream our lungs out from the sideline. Or if you'd rather get your mind off of it, maybe we can go somewhere. I hear the leaves around Silver Lake are a must-see right now."

She snorts. "And where did you hear that?"

"Internet."

She laughs again, which turns into a wince, and rolls her head back. "Well, I hate to spoil a trip I'm sure you've been looking forward to all year, but I'm not missing the game."

My limbs go taut, my head snapping to hers. Even as my stomach starts to roil, telling me everything I need to know, I have to clarify anyway. Because it can't be. She wouldn't put herself into harm's way like that. "So you want to watch from the bench together?"

She shifts her eyes to me slowly, the lids narrowed into slits, like I've asked the stupidest question in the history of questions. "Of course not. It's the championship. I've been working my butt off all season to get here. I have to play."

"Cate, you're injured." It comes out more condescending than I'd like, but seriously? I shouldn't have to say this at all. She has a *concussion.*

Pressing her palms flat against the plush couch cushion beneath her, she shifts to sit up a little farther. "I already told you, people get injured in this sport all the time. It's not a big deal. We play through it."

I match her movement, drawing my shoulders back. "Mindy said if you take one more hit to your nose that hairline crack will become a deviated septum." My voice sounds accusatory now, but I can't seem to rein it in.

She shakes her head. "Mindy was being overdramatic. I'm *fine*."

"What if you get hit again? What if it gets worse?" Again, the venom. I don't know why my volume is ratcheting up so high but I have no control over it. Someone else stole the remote, is messing with me from outside the front window. Blue emergency lights flash in my periphery, the gunshot ring of a metal gurney snapping into place echoes in my head. Towering spruces and pines sprout from the floor of Cate's living room, and suddenly I can't breathe.

"Paul," she bites out, and right away I recognize her use of my first name as a bad sign, but I'm too busy battling my own demons to care. "I know this is new for you, but it's par for the course in contact sports. If I stopped playing every time I *might* get hit again, I'd never run the field."

"Cate, it's just a game. We're talking about your health here."

As soon as the words leave my mouth, I have the good sense to regret them. Only by then, it's too late. She pulls her feet off my lap, twisting her body impossibly fast to tuck them underneath her. A rattlesnake recoiling.

"Just a game?" Her voice is already an octave higher than it was a minute ago. God, how I wish we could rewind to a minute ago. "Rugby isn't 'just a game' to me. On that field, my hard work means something. To so many other people. But it isn't even about them, it's about me. The moment I step onto that field, it doesn't matter what other people say or think about me. It doesn't matter what I did yesterday or the day before. When I'm out there, the rest of the world falls away. All that matters is that moment and what I make of it. It's *everything* to me."

I know I should listen more carefully, consider what she's telling me, what this new piece of her means in the broader spectrum of who Cate Seymour is. But my heart is beating erratically and the breaths I take are not nearly deep enough to fill my lungs. There's a poisonous mix of guilt and rage rising to a boil inside of me.

"I can't sit back and watch you beat yourself into the ground for other people. You're being completely irresponsible, Cate." I've managed to wrangle down my volume, but now my words are like ice. I'm every bit the guy she thought I was, the one she hated in those team meetings, but I can't turn it off. In fact, I'm clinging to it like a lifeline. The wall that's protected me for the last decade.

I sound like my father.

"Then don't!" The fuse I've been lighting finally explodes. Cate jumps to her feet and the knit blanket she was wearing falls to the floor, exposing her bare legs and the bruises on her thighs I should be used to by now. Some are new, others I've kissed in the quiet hours after midnight when it feels like magic is real. The memory cuts like a knife.

"I'm not going to shut down and change my entire life because of one bad thing, because of maybes and what ifs. Maybe that's okay for some people, but for me, that's unacceptable. It's worse than unacceptable. It's pathetic," she finishes in a rage.

My head jerks back like she's slapped me. Silence hangs in the room, a presence in its own right. The weight of it threatens to swallow me, swallow both of us, whole. Heavy enough to erase the last few weeks completely, send us back to when that's all there was between us: silence.

After a moment, she takes a tentative step forward and one hand reaches in my direction before it falls back to her side. "I shouldn't have—"

"I should go," I say, cutting her off. I unfold myself from the couch, holding up my palms between us. I can't meet her eyes. I don't want to go back to the way we were, but the bright walls, all these colorful knickknacks in her living room, the shadows of emergency responders I know aren't really there lurking in the corners, they're closing in on me. I have to get out.

"Paul," she breathes, but like me she doesn't know what to say. Our type, we don't know how to do this, the hard part. We never have.

Chapter 21

Cate

THE FLUORESCENT LIGHT OVERHEAD buzzes like a fly in my ear. I've never noticed the noise before, though I imagine it has always done this. My eyes stray from my computer monitors every few seconds to examine it, the tiniest flicker in the corner of the rectangular panel each time the buzz crescendos.

You blew it, it taunts. *No wonder no one wants to be around you.*

If I turn my head a fraction to the right and look as far as I can in my periphery, I can see his office. It's still dark. There's no buzzing sound behind its glass walls. No tap of fingers against a keyboard, no click of a cursor in an Excel sheet.

Just silence. What I should have been last Saturday.

I regretted the words as soon as they flew from my mouth. Not the message, not exactly. But the accusing tone. The way I'd called him pathetic.

Paul trusted me with a secret, the deepest one he has, and I threw it in his face.

He hasn't been back to work since.

I realize I'm now full-on staring at his empty office when Mindy's chair squeaks as it's pushed back from her desk. It makes me jump and duck my head closer to my keyboard, an artist's rendering of someone lost in their work.

It's fine, she doesn't notice me. Just stretching her legs. Her toes tap the bottom of her cubicle wall, making a little *thump* followed by a scraping sound.

Has the office always been this quiet? Why isn't the radio playing?

Right. I'm usually the one who turns it on in the morning.

I watch Mindy curl one leg underneath her on the absolutely-not-ergonomic VitaPop-issued chair—designed to be bright and fun-looking but most certainly not comfortable—and notice she has ear buds in. Good. Otherwise she might be able to hear my whirring thoughts, which would make her ask me why I've been staring at the same spreadsheet for thirty minutes.

The numbers jumble before my eyes every time I try to make sense of them. Over the past month, Paul has shown me brand new ways to use numbers: in my reports, in evaluating my financials, in my presentations. It seems only fitting the knowledge disappeared with him.

I feel my phone, sitting face down on the right side of my coffee thermos, more than I see it. It begs me to check it. *Flip it over, maybe a new message slipped past your constant vigilance.*

I must've texted him a hundred times. Not that first night, when I was still angry enough to think I'd been in the right. I'd hardly been able to sleep after, though. The guilt didn't take long to seep in, a cold presence in my room, a ghost watching me toss and turn.

I didn't have the heart to tell Mindy why he left when she got home from her parents' house, instead making some excuse about a family emergency. *Maybe that's where he is now*, I think darkly. His way of supporting me, even when we're fighting.

He hasn't responded to a single one of my texts or calls.

His office has been dark for the past three days.

Maybe he got sick, I'd thought on Monday. *Maybe he's working from home.*

But his icon on our company messaging app has been dark gray ever since. It's Wednesday afternoon now. I'm starting to doubt he'll be back at all this week.

I could probably ask around, find out where he is. Darius might know. But if I ask him and he doesn't already know, then he'd start asking around, and soon the entire office would get involved. Soon they'd all wonder: Why does Cate Seymour want to know where Paul Andrews is?

My cover, the project we'd been working on together, would fall apart under scrutiny. I'm sure of it. Maybe I shouldn't care. Maybe it's time for Paul and I to stop hiding what we are.

My throat dries. What if there's nothing to hide anymore? What if it's over?

Finally giving up on the spreadsheet, I close out of it and hop over to my email instead. The top five messages in there are all from Lauren Roth. The perfect distraction for my melancholy.

She's wonderful, like I knew she would be. Full of great ideas, very hands-on. She loves to "talk things out" which has made for a ton of emails. And phone calls, many of them after hours for me. But besides work and rugby practice, it's all I have to keep occupied.

I'm grateful for the six o'clock calls, the five a.m. "Oh! I had another thought" texts.

Her first post goes live on Monday, a day before CitraCrush launches in stores.

I should be angry at Paul for disappearing on me now. What if we hadn't filmed and edited enough drafts to get us through this week? It's freaking crunch time and now he decides to take a vacation?

He better be on an island somewhere, I think, welcoming the fiery heat that floods me. Anger is good. Anger is easier. *Because when I get my hands on him...*

Too quickly, it's gone. Replaced by a hollow sense of shame.

Mindy's voice breaks into the cage of my thoughts. "Have you started your Edie Awards application yet?"

I blink, my computer screen dimming before my eyes. A warning it hasn't been getting enough attention in a while and wants to sleep. *You and me both, sister.*

The awards. I haven't thought about them in weeks, since the last time Mindy asked. The hollowness grows. At first, I didn't think I'd be able to apply at all. The entire idea had hinged on winning in the influencer marketing category. One influencer, even if it is Lauren Roth, would hardly be enough to upset the other candidates.

I'd told Mindy as much one night in our cramped living room, our chopsticks digging into the leftover bibimbap her mom made. Without hesitation, she'd pulled up the list of awards on her phone and showed me two other categories I could try for: Best of Social Media Video and Most Engagement in Social Media.

At the time, I'd eagerly grabbed the phone from her, dropping my chopsticks to the coffee table, rice spilling onto the scuffed surface. My head spun with the possibilities.

That was the last time it crossed my mind, until now. Spinning a half-turn in my chair, I give Mindy the smallest shake of my head. "Not yet." *Not ever.* It's strange how quickly something I thought I wanted so badly can seem so inconsequential.

She purses her lips, corners turned down. Her eyes feel like an X-ray, probing for what's just beneath my surface. "The deadline is in two weeks."

"Things have been crazy lately. It slipped my mind," I dodge. "I'll get to it." Another lie. Why am I lying? More importantly, why don't I want this anymore?

I can tell Mindy's not placated. She stares me down a few more seconds, then reluctantly offers a half smile and a shallow nod. Whatever she saw in my expression, she decided now was not the time nor the place to prod. Safe until tonight, at home, where I'm sure she'll find a way to bring it up again.

I could apply. I should, even. Our content, though not at all what I set out to do, is unique. Engaging. Award-worthy.

But at some point while working with Paul, I stopped caring about that. It wasn't why we were doing this. Sure, I wanted our posts to perform well, but not to stand up under the scrutiny of some arbitrary pool of judges.

This was about us. About finding our audience and entertaining them, while hopefully selling a few cans of soda along the way. I don't need an award to tell me our content is good. I don't need anyone else to prove that what we've been doing matters. I already know that. Can feel it in the way my stomach flips when Paul and I watch the replay on something we filmed. Can see it in the way his face lights up when he has a new idea we just have to shoot *today*. That feeling, of being onto something, being excited about something new and unfamiliar, not knowing if it's going to be great or a total disaster, that's what made this project special. Not external validation—although the hundreds of thousands of views didn't hurt my ego.

My breath catches in my throat. A memory resurfaces, me in my car on my way to a scrimmage. My mom, silent as a cemetery on speaker phone. The fear, the disappointment, then the familiar resignation that followed.

Another memory, me pacing outside the VitaPop office in a horrendously vibrant ugly Christmas sweater of my own design. My dad's voice in my ear, telling me he and Mom decided to go on a cruise with my brother Brian and his wife instead of coming to visit me in Seattle. The realization I'll likely be spending the holiday alone hitting me like a Mack truck.

And finally, a third memory, this time in the too-bright test kitchen, light flooding in from the wall-to-wall windows on one side of the room. I hover over Paul at the bar-height counter. I tell him not to live his life according to what others want, what others expect, because you can't depend on them and their desires to find happiness. You can only find that in yourself.

I hadn't made the connection at the time, drawn the parallels between how he chose to live his life and the hope I'd been clinging to for so long. Not until now, when I can see the way our time together changed me.

The Cate standing there in the test kitchen was right, and it's time I took her advice. It's time to let go of that little girl, the one caught in the middle, desperate for attention from tired parents who had nothing left to give her.

I'll probably never stop wanting their approval. All children are hardwired that way, I think. It's a survival instinct leftover from the caveman days.

But *I* don't need it to survive. I don't have to prove anything to anyone else.

Paul's fear for me when we argued the other night may have come from a dark place, but he was right. I don't have to pummel myself into the ground to be worth something.

CHaPTer 22

Paul

THE ARMPITS OF MY starchy, white button-down shirt are already damp, sticking uncomfortably to my skin. Thankfully I opted to wear a suit jacket, the thick, black wool covering up my anxiety like a shield.

It's unseasonably warm for the last week of September in Eugene, Oregon. Most of the men around me have already sloughed off their extra layers, abandoned in car passenger seats on the way here or on one of the folding chairs lined up in neat rows in the backyard.

Jake's backyard. Or at least it used to be.

My throat threatens to close. Wouldn't that be something? If I keeled over at his memorial. *Sorry, bud. Couldn't let you have all the attention!*

What a morbid thought. There must be something wrong with me.

My mom squeezes my elbow from behind. She knows how hard this is. How long I've avoided this exact situation, and why. The tiny application of pressure says *it's okay. You're doing fine.* My father is over her shoulder, deep in conversation with another man. I don't recall his name, only that he had a daughter in my grade. I can't remember her name either, but I think she was on the basketball team.

I recognize a few of the faces ahead of us in the buffet line, kids from high school and their parents. Bethany is with them, head bent toward someone in front of her. I can't see who it is, just a brown ponytail bobbing in the air. My cousin kept her roots in this town even after moving away while I ripped mine out at the source.

They're not kids anymore, I remind myself. And neither am I, though being back here, after how cowardly I've been the past ten years, it's hard to think I'm anything but.

I haven't seen any of these people since the funeral. I wonder if I look different to them. I wonder if they remember me.

The line moves slowly, winding around the Turners' dining room, but soon I'm digging silver tongs into a giant bowl of garden salad and heaving the leafy greens onto my plate. I won't be able to eat them, but at least they'll help me fit in.

A salad of purpose. Something to do here, other than have a panic attack.

I pick up a spoonful of baked ziti. Mrs. Turner's specialty. My mouth twitches for the first time since I entered her house, one I'd spent so many days and nights in so many years ago. She used to make it every Sunday and either by divine intervention or a growling stomach, I'd find my way here for dinner. My mom was a good cook, still is I'm sure. But there was something about Mrs. Turner's ziti.

With a knowing grin, Jake had once elbowed me in the ribs and confided she made it especially for me. The second son she'd always wanted but never had.

The guilt creeps in again, like whispering shadows lurking right outside my field of vision. I should've stayed home. I should've come back sooner.

I blink and I'm through the buffet line, unsure where to go from here. Though we're years past it, the memorial is just like high school: cliques weaving their way back together, heads bent toward one another across picnic tables, hushed conversations and darting eyes.

A celebration of life, Mrs. Turner called it in her voicemail. Jake would've liked that. "A memorial sounds like something for stuffy old people," he'd say, dimples dancing.

If he'd had the foresight to make a will at the ripe old age of eighteen, he'd have probably asked for a zipline at his funeral. I snort under my breath, and my mom lifts an eyebrow in my direction. Steeling my face back to neutral, I follow her outside to a set of three folding chairs already turned toward each other. My dad finally stopped his turn around the room to rejoin us in time for lunch.

I've managed to eat two bites of ziti and pushed my salad around so much that the oil in the dressing is starting to separate when a small voice says from over my shoulder, "Paul?"

Ten years and I'd still recognize it anywhere.

I stand, nearly dropping my plastic plate to the ground in the process. "Mrs. Turner." The first syllable of her name comes out like a cough.

I've always been taller than her—well, since my growth spurt in the tenth grade at least—but she seems smaller than I remember.

There are wrinkles around her eyes, deep lines carved around the corners of her mouth that weren't there the last time I saw her.

It's a relief to see them, one I hadn't anticipated. They're the body armor of someone who met tragedy head on and lived enough beyond it to find laughter. Canyons carved by little rivers of joy, no matter how small or slow their trickle. How infrequent.

"Please, I think it's high time you called me Amber." The smile she wears is small but welcoming. Meant to put me at ease. I release a breath and try to mirror it, probably unsuccessfully.

"Mind if I borrow your son for a few minutes?" she asks my parents, laying a tender hand on my forearm.

After I rise, she leads me to a far corner of the yard. When I lived around the block, it was nothing but a patch of grass that got too much sun in the summer, turning the entire area brown no matter what Mr. Turner did. Now I see Amber's planted a garden here, under the shade of a large willow. A bench at the garden's heart bears Jake's initials, scrawled in polished gold cursive. It's beautiful, but I'm grateful she doesn't ask me to sit on it.

She takes up a position on a flagstone path leading through the center of the garden and folds her arms around her middle. I keep about a foot away, hands tucked into my pockets, body angled toward hers.

"How have you been?"

I freeze, stumped by the first question. What's the right answer? Fine is too shallow. Perfunctory, bordering on rude. But good feels like it's rubbing her face in it.

I'm alive. Who cares how I've been? Shouldn't that be enough?

Against my better judgment, and just before too much time has passed, I settle for, "I've been good. How have you been?"

She nods. "Good, good." She seems distracted now, her reason for searching me out evaporating like dew on a July morning. Her head bobs a little too fast, her fingers pick at one another in front of her stomach, her eyes dart around. Finally, she stops shuffling and meets my gaze. Pierces it is more like it. It takes everything in me not to recoil.

"Look, there's no right way to bring this up, but I've been wanting to talk to you for—gosh, years I suppose—and doing it over a call or text didn't feel right. Now you're here, well, I'm going to get on with it." She takes a deep breath, her small shoulders rising and falling. "I get the sense from—" her eyes drift momentarily across the yard, to where my parents are still sitting on folding chairs. "Well, I get the sense you've been beating yourself up a bit. Since Jakey passed."

This must be what people feel like when they've been punched. All the wind is knocked out of me.

I picture Mrs. Turner—Amber—sitting at the small table in my parents' breakfast nook, dissecting my life choices over piping hot Folgers from the Mr. Coffee my dad refuses to replace and cookies from the grocery store. "He has a good job, a decent apartment, a safe car—all the things I'm supposed to want for him. But I don't know if he's happy," my mom says in this fantasy, blowing across the top of her mug to cool the brown liquid.

My shock must register on my face, because Amber immediately reaches out with both hands and gently grasps my wrists. "I don't mean to pry, sweetheart. We all grieve in our own ways, in our own time. I understand that better than most."

She gives me a soft pat-pat with her fingertips, then drops her arms to her sides, then crosses them at her middle. She purses her lips and then puffs them out in a breath. All the while, I remain a deer in the headlights. Any slight movement will give it away. What "it" is, I'm not exactly sure, only that I don't want to be caught out.

"Mariam says you stopped making videos," she says, now referencing my mom outright. To anyone else, this shift would seem like a non sequitur. I see it for what it truly is: a tactic change.

I nod, wary.

A weak gust of wind makes the willow tree dance beside us. Amber watches it and smiles to herself. She's a little bit taller when she turns back to me and leans in conspiratorially to whisper, "I still watch them sometimes, you know. The ones you and Jake made in high school."

I blink, surprised. They're all still on YouTube—I couldn't bring myself to take them down. It would've required looking at them, and looking at them is a small step away from watching them, which is something I couldn't do. Wouldn't do. Haven't done.

I guess deep down I always knew the occasional person might stumble across them and give them a watch. Heck, if someone had a sprinkle of willpower and my full name, they could find them outright after a little searching. My mind drifts to Cate, wondering if she ever did. She's so curious, my story probably making her even more so.

"When something happens that reminds me of Jake, or on his birthday, or, heck I can admit it, sometimes when I'm missing him deeply for no reason other than I'm his mother and that's what mothers do," Amber is saying now, her gaze soft and pointed at the middle distance, "I'll pull up his old account on my tablet and lose myself for hours."

Her smile turns wistful when she adds, "Every time I do, I'm floored by how many you both made. How talented you were." She snaps her eyes back to mine and I try not to flinch. "Out of all of them, you know which one is my favorite?"

I suck in a breath and hold it while I shake my head. There are dozens from back then, maybe even a hundred, but my stomach twists because I already know which one she's going to—

"The old watering hole, the one that forks off a tributary of the Willamette River." She laughs under her breath and shakes her head, something I haven't seen—that I've tried not to think about for a decade—playing through her mind. "You two went to so many places, across the country, across the world—" Her bottom lip trembles on the last word. "But my favorite one to watch is from right here in our backyard."

I know it well, the video she's talking about. A hundred years couldn't make me forget. It wasn't our first video, nor our last. It wasn't a particularly interesting location; everyone in Eugene knows about it.

There is nothing notable about that video, except that it's my favorite too. And if I had asked Jake back then—there's so many things I wish I had asked him—I think he'd agree.

I can still hear his voice, his laugh, while he climbed halfway up the twisted limbs of the old western juniper beside the water and grabbed the sun-bleached rope that has dangled from its boughs since long before either of us was born. "I'm gonna do a double backflip, make sure you get it."

One corner of my mouth turns up. He did not, in fact, do a double backflip. He barely made it one turn around in the air before he crashed down into the water, mostly on his stomach.

"I see you remember it," Amber says, bringing me back to reality. There's a sparkle in her eyes that wasn't there before.

"He got right back up and tried again," I murmur, like she's been in my thoughts this whole time. Like she's seen what I've seen in the replay. I didn't have the heart to include his second attempt in the video. It was even worse than the first.

She replies without missing a beat, "Oh, I believe it. The first time we took him to Dixon's, when he was nine years old, we couldn't get him off the rope swing."

I chuckle and it feels like taking a small pick to a sheet of ice: a tentative tap, a little pressure, to lodge the first crack in the thick slab. One more tap and breathing gets easier. A few more and, well, maybe it will break apart altogether.

Amber touches my elbow, drawing me back to her. Her eyes are shiny, little blue reflecting pools. "Every time I watch those videos, I feel closer to my son. I get to relive some of his best memories, memories I wouldn't have access to, if it hadn't been for you.

"You gave me a gift, and now I want to give you one." A single tear spills from the corner of her left eye, and a prickle like I've inhaled salt water stings the back of my nose. "What happened on that mountain wasn't your fault. It was no one's fault." Her words are a whisper I can barely hear, quieter than the passing breeze, and yet they buzz loudly in my head as though she'd spoken through a megaphone.

It's the second time someone has told me this in as many weeks, but the repetition doesn't dull the impact. When I close my eyes, it forces the first tears to fall. I let Amber envelop me in a tight embrace, her grip strong for such a small woman, and my arms carefully fold around her.

"Please forgive yourself, Paul," she says against my chest, and I roll my lips between my teeth to keep it together.

"I'll try," I croak, and for the first time in a long time, possibly ever, I mean it. I *want* to, more than I've ever wanted anything before.

My legs are burning by the time this trail opens up to the rocky cliffside. A few days a week on a treadmill are no match for the hills of Eugene. I need to get out more.

Hiking. Another thing I've avoided since Jake's passing.

I think of Cate, what she'd say if she knew, and smile. Within twenty-four hours, she'd probably have a full itinerary planned for us. Every weekend filled with hikes along trails in and around Seattle.

It only took me a day to forgive her, for what she'd said to me. Less, if I'm honest with myself. It had stung, and it was blunt, but she had been right. In that insufferable way of hers, she had stripped me bare and shone a light on the parts of me I never wanted anyone else to see.

She'd called me on my bullshit.

That's when I knew I needed to come back here. That I couldn't answer any of her hundred apology texts or calls until I did. Until I faced it head on and could return to her, not entirely whole yet, but on track to be the kind of man she deserves. That we both deserve.

Though I've stopped now, the sun is still climbing, washing the outcrop in a pale-yellow light. I have to squint to see through it after an hour in the dark cocoon of trees that hug the trail. I raise my hand to my forehead, makeshift shade, and look out over the valley. The crisp autumn air fills my lungs, pushing them full to bursting, until I let it out again.

It's my first time here in more than ten years and it's more beautiful than I remembered. The peaks are still bathed in plenty of green, even in late September, from the towering deciduous varieties that call this forest home. The bigleaf maples are the star of the show, though, resplendent in gold.

And at right after seven in the morning, it's all mine. Tourists will fill this outcrop, clog up the trail, in less than an hour. But for now, it's just me. And the reason I came here.

Last night, my old laptop from high school sounded like a helicopter about to take off when I booted it up. I was only fifty percent sure the device wouldn't explode on my lap and set fire to my parents' den. Fortunately, it held out long enough for my mission.

I couldn't get Amber's words out of my head for the rest of the day. They spoke to me, a phantom voice, on the drive back to my parents' house. They whispered to me as I paced the worn blue carpet of my childhood bedroom. They beckoned to me over dinner, which I scarfed down like an animal after passing on lunch.

Finally, I couldn't take it anymore. The old computer had been right where I'd left it, though it took far longer than it used to to turn on and open a browser tab.

I started my journey through time with my favorite video, but I didn't stop there. I didn't stop until hours had passed and big droplets of salt water covered the keyboard.

I wasn't sad. Or at least, I wasn't *only* sad. My cheeks hurt from smiling. My voice rasped from laughing. The muscles in my legs twitched, aching like I was back out there: scaling down the valley to Dixon's watering hole; following the thin trails near Cascade Locks; slipping in mud to see the white-tipped peak of Mount Hood after a particularly rainy season.

I never posted any of the videos we took in Europe. The plan had always been to edit them at home together, when I had access to all my equipment. When there was no us, no *together* anymore, I couldn't bring myself to do it alone.

Maybe I should dig up the footage, I had thought to myself in the dense quiet, the kind you only experience in the middle of the night, when no one else is awake. *Another time,* a friendly voice whispered in my head. *Baby steps.* It sounded eerily like Cate.

That was when my dad found me down there. When I first saw him, hovering in the doorway, I froze. And then I realized what I'd really been doing all these years, each time I turned into the statue. I was bracing myself, waiting for the other shoe to drop. Since Jake passed, I'd been living my life that way, constantly afraid of the next big hurt. Desperate to avoid it.

"You watching those old videos?" my dad asked, joining me on the couch, and I bristled. He must've noticed the way my shoulders bunched, because he laid a gentle hand on one, weighing it back into place. After a deep sigh that drew my attention he said, "I know I was hard on you, about your future. I wanted what every parent wants: for you to have a good life, a better life. And I was afraid of what might happen if you didn't get it."

My throat had gone dry, listening to him. He explained how Jake, what happened to him, made him even more afraid. How relieved he'd been when I went to school for finance, got a safe and secure job in accounting. How that same fear had resurfaced, unexpectedly, when my cousin Bethany sent him and my mom the video of me.

At the time, he didn't understand it, his fear. Like I couldn't understand mine either.

We'd been living with it this whole time. Maybe to different degrees and for different reasons, but it was the same fear inside both of us nonetheless, eating us alive, keeping us apart.

"You look happier now," he told me with a small smile. "And you're finally home, heaven knows your mom is over the moon about that." I'd chuckled, the sound a little choked and wet. He paused to hold my gaze for a few long moments, our navy eyes mirror images of one another. "If this is what helps you heal," he'd said, before retreating from the room, "then heal."

When I reach the final summit of my climb now, there's a boulder not far from the cliff's edge, worn smooth from thousands of hands and feet. I take a seat on it, leaving space to my right, like always. The sun has claimed its perch in the sky and warms my upturned face. Somewhere far off in the distance, a woodpecker gets to work on a tree trunk, the staccato *tap-tap-tap* echoing over the canyon below.

My lungs rattle on my next breath. The morning is almost perfectly clear, the sky a rich cerulean you can only appreciate from up high in places like this. A gift from Jake, I think.

The words are a barely-audible jumble when I finally muster enough courage to say them out loud, but I know he can hear them as well as if he were next to me. "I'm sorry I haven't been around. For a while, it was too hard. And I was too selfish. Too ashamed."

I tell him I miss him. That I sometimes wonder what he might think of me now, if he'd be proud or disappointed in the life I've built. I've done so much that would disappoint Jake, I think. But I want to do better, starting now. I'm ready.

Trees rustle on the next peak over and then a bald eagle bursts through the branches. Its wings are angled on the breeze as it carves a path up, up, up. I smile as it disappears toward the horizon. A sign he's here. He's listening.

"I met someone," I confess. "You'd love her." And I mean it, he would. I tell Jake all about Cate. How beautiful she is, and headstrong too. How she hated me until recently, which for some reason makes me ache for her even more now. How, even when she said one of the most devastating things I've ever had to hear—because I did have to hear it—I knew she was right. And though it hurt, I loved her even more for it.

I stay there with Jake until the first tourists' voices reach my ears from a few yards down the trail. When I begin my descent, I know what I need to do next.

CHAPTER 23

Cate

I SWIPE MY HAND at a piece of hair that fell out of my ponytail and drifted into my eyes and follow my teammates along the grassy trail to the pitch. A lone ray of sunlight streaks its way through a patch of clouds the color of ash. The heavy mass seems to be moving closer and closer to the ground, sucking any warmth out of the air. On a deep inhale, an earthy scent fills my nose, and an involuntary shiver rakes up my spine. Fall in Seattle, beautiful but fickle.

The crowd is thick. I can tell by the sound of people talking and cheering behind me. I resist the urge to turn around and scan the faces for someone familiar. I'm glad people showed up for my team, but I know no one's up there for me.

And that's okay.

Last year, an empty bench where I so desperately wanted my parents to be almost broke me. This year, the thought of it still stings, but less. It's like Coach always says: "Progress, not perfection."

The championship game. We made it. I touch a finger gingerly to the bridge of my nose and wince at the pressure. Though I no longer look like I lost a bar fight in a Tarantino film, it's still bruised and tender. My doctor offered me a prescription for the pain, but I declined. The reminder is good. The reminder of all I've accomplished, what I made it through to get here. The reminder of what I need to do today.

I join my team for a group stretch, keeping my back to the stands. It feels good, pushing my muscles almost to the breaking point in a deep lunge. Coach is saying something inspirational to us, trying to get the team fired up, but it goes in one of my ears and out the other.

Those words aren't meant for me.

The hard metal of the silver bench beside the pitch is even colder than the air when I slide onto it and watch my team jog onto the field without me.

I'm not sure when I made the decision not to play today. It wasn't at the radiologist. I'd smiled and nodded politely while the doctor talked to me about the risks. My nose isn't broken enough to need surgery now, but it's about a hair away from it. One more good hit and I'd be done for, she'd warned.

It certainly hadn't been the night it happened, the night I fought with Paul. I'd been so damn sure of myself then, so determined to be here, to do this.

But at some point between then and now, I decided that maybe his advice hadn't been so stupid. That maybe his fear had been warranted.

Now I'm a bench warmer. Lovely. I blame Paul Andrews.

At least some things haven't changed.

A soft voice carries my name on the breeze and the back of my neck prickles. Stiff from more couch surfing than I'm used to, I slowly turn to scan the crowd, the one thing I told myself I wouldn't do. The voice was probably in my head. I don't recognize any of these faces.

Until, there—a head of long, black hair bounces underneath a knit beanie as she waves. Mindy. My chest warms at the sight of her beaming like she just spotted her celebrity crush. I'd told her not to come, but as she wolf whistles around two fingers—I still have no idea how she can do that—and yells my name, I'm so glad she ignored me.

The sky behind her is even darker and I try not to frown. A little bit of rain they'll play through, but a storm would call the game. I give her a quick wave and turn back to the game about to start, trying to ward off the tingle in the back of my sinuses. Within minutes of the whistle, the first ruck forms on the ground, both teams struggling to move the ball to freedom. One of my teammates manages to secure it and the game moves on.

I try to follow it but my eyes glaze over, my head heavy like the sky, clouded with things I wish I could ignore. Like it has been every day at work, and every day at home too. Without the game to focus on now, the unwanted thoughts creep in.

As expected, my parents are no-shows. I confirmed it before turning away from Mindy. It's not a surprise, my mom said as much on the phone the other day. It's for the best.

If they were here, my choice would've been that much harder. Risk the disappointment in their eyes when they realize, after a ten-hour drive, I'm warming the bench, or risk another head injury, one that could end my playing days for good—or worse?

I know what I'd have picked. If my parents were here, I'd be on that field right now. I look up right as one of my teammates, Corinne, is tackled to the ground. The hit was clean, her head protected from the brunt of the fall, but it still makes me cringe. My nose twinges in answer.

Minutes later, the crowd erupts behind me, feet pounding on the steel bleachers and shouts echoing through cupped fingers. I startle then scan the field, holding my breath until I find our team in the try zone—we scored!

I scrabble to my feet, punching one arm into the air in front of my chest. My breath releases in a walloping cheer. From what little I watched of the game so far, it's obvious the other team is good. To get on the board this quickly is a good sign for my girls.

Our best kicker picks up the conversion and the two teams move to the halfway line for kickoff, the crowd quieting down to follow the progression of the game. I keep my eyes on the ball, trying to focus on the calls of my teammates to one another, their grunts, the practiced rhythm they move in. With only the sound of my breath whistling in and out of my nose to keep me company, I remind myself it's okay for them to succeed without me. It doesn't mean I'm not important. It means I've done my job, we all have. A team that collapses under one absence isn't a team at all.

The thought makes me smile, makes my shoulders loosen. The metal bench underneath me doesn't feel quite as cold anymore.

After a few plays and a score from the opposing team, the droplets start to fall. A light sprinkle, you'd barely notice it if you weren't sitting still. I try to ignore it anyway, balling my hands into fists against the tops of my thighs, watching my team like a hawk as we move down the field. The crowd erupts after another score and my throat burns from screaming right along with them.

With each play, each score, it gets easier to cheer them on from the sidelines. It reminds me of Paul that day in the staff meeting when I presented the reports he made. How happy he'd been to watch me succeed, with no desire for the spotlight. I smile down at myself, sending a rogue raindrop splattering from my forehead onto my legs. I wish he were here. Wish I'd heard from him.

The noise of the crowd dies down again, but this time there's a low chant still coursing from behind me. It's quiet, one voice instead of a sea of many. I can barely make it out from this far away, through the wind now starting to whip the droplets sideways.

But then another voice joins it and—it sounds like my name.

Slowly, I crane my neck around, scanning the stands for the source. I have to shield my eyes with my hand to block the thickening streaks of rain picking up speed as they fall from above. The small pieces of hair that frame my face are now plastered to it.

My mouth drops open, eyes widening. Dead center in the crowd stands a lanky man with damp sandy blond hair flopping over his forehead. On his left hand, he wears a comically large, royal blue foam finger. It flaps and dances with every pump of his arm.

His other hand is cupped around his mouth, and now that I've laid eyes on him, it's crystal clear. He *is* calling my name. Shouting it over and over at the top of his lungs like an idiot.

I cover the bottom half of my face with a hand, trying to hide the flush stretching across my cheeks and the grin breaking out across my lips. I have to tear my eyes away from his face, his impossibly handsome face, and that's when I notice it. The white jersey with royal blue lettering he's wearing. My number emblazoned across his chest.

Even from thirty feet away, I can see the beaming grin on Paul's face, just before he turns around. He hooks the thumb of his non-foam-fingered hand and aims it at a spot between his shoulder blades. There, in big, block lettering, sits my last name.

And now both of my hands are covering my face, my nose stinging from both the pressure and the salt water threatening to spill from my eyes. For the first time, I notice Mindy beside him, screaming her damn head off and pointing at his jersey. Like I could've missed it otherwise.

A laugh mixed with a croaking sob racks through my chest, and then I'm standing. And then I'm running, running faster than I ever have toward the bleachers, sneakers slipping in the wet grass threatening to turn to mud.

Paul meets me at the bottom of the steel steps, snatching me up in his arms. His chest is impossibly warm as I crush my face into it, ignoring the sting of pain that erupts from my nose. His arms are like a vice, unrelenting, holding me together.

The tears I've been holding back finally spill, but his jersey absorbs them right along with the rain. One more way Paul lets me know it's okay, without even trying.

Reluctantly, I pull back to look at him, fat raindrops peppering my face in the process. It's pouring now, but the sound of the game still carries on behind me. No thunder yet. "You're wearing my jersey," I rasp, and it sounds so stupid when there are so many other things I want to say to him.

He just smiles, lifting a hand to brush a piece of soaked hair from my eyes. "You deserve to have someone cheering for you, always."

Before his words can sink in, I'm shaking my head, poised to disagree. Old habits die hard. "Paul, what I said to you—"

He cuts me off with a soft kiss. He's so careful not to put any pressure on my nose. Damn superhero. Against my lips, he whispers, "I needed to hear it."

I open my mouth to protest when someone beside us in the bleachers clears their throat. There's an old man on the end of a row, the hood of a windbreaker pulled low over his eyes, shooting us daggers. A few seats down from him, Mindy looks like she's about to jump the poor guy on our behalf. Paul and I grimace at one another, realizing at the same time that perhaps the bleachers aren't the best place for a reunion. Whatever we might be, to ourselves or to each other, we are not the PDA type.

I drag him by the hand down the remaining five steps and around the back of the bleachers, by the fence that marks the entrance to the field, for more privacy. Craning my neck to look into Paul's eyes, I ask, "Where have you been?"

I'm still holding his hand, like if I let go he might float away and disappear. The foam finger is missing from his other, lost during our flight. It's probably laying in wet grass, soaking up water like a sponge.

After seeing Paul at a rugby game, wearing my jersey and screaming my name, I didn't think anything else could shock me. When he tells me he drove back to Eugene to attend a memorial for his friend who passed away, I stand corrected.

"You were right, Cate," he says at the end of his story, giving both of my hands a little squeeze. "After Jake died, I shut down."

As elated as I am to hear this, to see his willingness to confront his pain, the way I spoke to him last weekend drags me down like an anchor. Apologies don't come easily to me, they never have, but he deserves one. "No, I wasn't right. I shouldn't have said that, I—"

He bends down until his face is almost level with mine. His navy eyes are the brightest I've ever seen them. "Maybe how you said it was a little blunt." At this I can't help but sniff a laugh, partly because it's the understatement of the year and partly because he says it in a tone that screams *you wouldn't be you if you hadn't*. "But you *were* right. I've been avoiding that part of my life for so long, not realizing it's not some external thing I could put in a box and stow away to forget. I've been avoiding the things that make me *me*.

"You made me see that, Cate." When he presses his lips to mine again, I can taste my tears mixed with the rain. "If you hadn't been so belligerent about it, I probably wouldn't have listened," he teases against my lips.

A watery laugh bubbles out of me, and I shake my head even as I cup his face gently in my hands, stroking his high cheekbones with my thumbs. We've never touched one another so openly before. Because of work and because of all we were hiding from one another. Compartmentalizing. After a week apart, we can't keep our hands off each other.

"Why aren't you out there?" Paul lifts his chin toward the field, the rugby game still going on. We can't see it from our hiding place, but we can hear it.

I incline my chin, mouth twisting to hide a crooked smile. "Oh, some guy told me playing today was a death wish and I should maybe sit this one out."

Paul strokes a hand through my hair, eyebrows raised. "And you listened to him?"

With a shrug, I say, "He seemed to know what he was talking about."

He hums. "I don't know, sounds like a giant know-it-all with a superiority complex to me."

There's no hiding my answering smile, even as water runs down my face in rivulets. You could see it from space. I slide my hand around the back of his neck to pull him closer and whisper, "Nah, he's okay," just before I press my lips to his.

I don't tell him he was right. I don't have to. He knows what it means for me to give up playing in the championship game, what it took me to get here. I can feel it in the way his skin warms in my hands, the way his mouth tastes, the surety with which he holds me.

We'll talk about it, eventually. What it means for both of us to heal, how to do it together. We'll talk about what together means, the other elephant we've ignored in the room. But not today.

We're like two teenagers cutting class, hands roving over each other's backs and sides, tongues exploring one another's mouths. After what could be minutes or hours, Paul pulls back, breathless. Water runs off the tip of his nose and splatters against my chin. "This is all so exciting," he whispers. "I've never cheered for a bench warmer before."

Without any force, I swat his chest, brushing against the vinyl number 43 there. My number. I grab the collar of the jersey, the material soft in my hand, and pull him down to me again.

EPILOGUE

Paul

Three months later

"Told you you'd be famous one day," Cate murmurs under her breath from my side, and my lips sweep into a smile.

"Actually, you said you hoped we'd *both* be famous soon," I correct in a low voice without turning to her. Aside from these few whispered words, the two of us look like we're in a trance, eyes trained on the wide flat screen TV in front of us.

It's mounted proudly to the shelf at one end of a Whole Foods Market aisle, playing the stop-motion-style commercial I created a few months ago for CitraCrush on a loop. A prime spot toward the front of the store, cases of our sodas organized in neat little rows across four shelves below it.

I'd never finished typing that email to Darius, never pressed send. After Cate got hurt and we fought, it slipped through the cracks.

Though if I'm being honest, I never intended to send it. I was only going through the motions. For her.

Cate bumps her hip against mine when the video starts over and drags her eyes to me. Without thinking twice about it, I catch her waist, slide my arm around it until she's tucked against my side, her head fitting perfectly into the spot where my shoulder meets my neck.

She's the reason my work now plays in nearly eighty Whole Foods Markets up and down the western seaboard. Where I failed, she picked up the torch, showing it to Darius *behind my back*. Eight months ago, I'd have been angry about that. Then again, eight months ago there wouldn't have even been a commercial.

Without Cate, there wouldn't be a lot of things.

Which is why I've decided to pay her back in kind. Thanks to Mindy and the power of caffeine, I managed to submit an application to the Edie Awards on Cate's behalf at 11:59 the evening they were due. It's a feat in itself that I was able to get a night away to work on it without her prying eyes. Since the new soda launched, we've seen quite a bit of each other.

A forwarded copy of the email the committee sent me announcing her as a finalist should hit her inbox Monday morning.

I angle my head to look at her now, trying to pull down the corners of my mouth without success. I'm afraid she'll read it on my face, what I'm hiding in my thoughts. Keeping it from her, trying not to think about it when she's around, has become a second job.

At VitaPop, I've continued helping her out in small ways even though our required time together is over. Sometimes it's with budget planning—our partnership with the influencer Lauren Roth paid off with a huge spike in sales immediately following the CitraCrush launch. Cate, being Cate, has already strong-armed it into a larger marketing budget. Every once in a while, I get to work on a video with her too.

Darius even offered me an open position on the marketing team. I politely declined. I still love numbers, and there are plenty of stories left for me to tell with data. That and I'm not sure what spending 24/7 with Cate would be like for our relationship. We'd either create a hive mind or kill one another. I'm no betting man, and I'm not ready to take those odds.

Spending almost every weekend with her is more than I could ask for. For now.

"I think I liked it better when you two were sneaking around," says a wry voice from behind us, and my fingers twitch against Cate's hip. "Now you're insufferable."

Cate leans up to plant a dramatic, wet kiss to my cheek before sliding out of my grip and turning to her best friend Mindy standing there. She's toting a small, black, plastic basket with at least four bottles of wine in it. Two white and two red. Cate and I lift our brows in unison.

"It's my contribution to family dinner," she offers, shifting the basket and sending the bottles rolling against one another. "You know I can't cook," she adds, glancing pointedly to Cate.

"And here I thought you came all the way to Belltown to see my work on display," I interject, earning a smile from both women. Spending so many evenings (and mornings) at Cate's place, I've gotten to know Mindy almost as well as her roommate. I don't want to jinx it, but I think we may have actually become friends in the process.

Mindy scoffs and props the heavy basket against her hip, but her eyes dance in the fluorescent light overhead. "Let's just say there's a market about fifteen minutes closer to our house that I drove by to get here."

I tilt my head to the floor to hide my smile while Cate gives my hand a squeeze.

We follow Mindy a few yards to the only open checkout lane and, once she's loaded her wine onto the conveyor belt, snag her empty basket for ourselves and say our goodbyes. With the basket in one hand and Cate's hand in my other, we head for the snack aisle.

Today is a big day. Even if a video I produced wasn't playing for thousands of shoppers, today would be a big day.

Today, Cate is making the four-hour drive to Eugene with me to meet my parents. She won't admit it to me, and I shouldn't expect otherwise, but I can tell she's nervous by the way her fingers twitch against mine every few steps.

Our sides bump occasionally as we head down the colorful aisle, scanning the shelves for whatever vibrant box or bag filled with heart-attack-inducing snacks might catch our eye.

If your road trip snack haul doesn't look like you set a pair of children loose in a gas station, you're doing it wrong. That's what Cate told me on our way here, at least.

Without a word, she tosses a box of Nature Valley Sweet & Salty Nut bars into my basket. I give her a sidelong glance from the corner of my eye that says *too healthy* then top it with a family-size bag of Cool Ranch Doritos. She doesn't look up, but I see the tilt at the corner of her mouth. Her fingers finally stop their twitching.

Between us we add a king-size package of Reese's Peanut Butter Cups, a can of Sour Cream & Onion Pringles, and two Slim Jims to the basket, then make our way to the checkout. There's no way we'll eat even half this in four hours, but I don't think that's the point.

The last time I made this drive, I was a wreck.

My heart ached from my fight with Cate. It ached for Mr. and Mrs. Turner, for what they've endured the last ten years. It ached for what I'd done, abandoning the second family who'd never once turned me away.

It ached for what I'd lost on that mountain in Germany, and for what I'd given up afterward too.

Today, Cate is determined to give me a different experience. To unlock a new core memory. And it makes my heart ache for a totally different and significantly more pleasant reason.

As I slide my credit card through the reader, the small weight in the left breast pocket of my flannel shirt beats against my chest. Or maybe it's the thud of my own heart, hammering against it, that I feel. Absentmindedly, I pat it with my free hand, feel the sharp ridged outline of the single gold key in there.

Cate doesn't know it yet, but the lease on my shoebox apartment is up next month. Instead of renewing for a fourth year in a row, I decided to find a larger, less shabby apartment. In Arbor Heights.

She also doesn't know we'll be making a small pit stop there before driving to Eugene.

I don't expect her to up and move in with me, not yet. Besides, there's at least another five months on her rental agreement with Mindy. But I want her to know that I'm ready to let her in. That I want to be closer to her, even if it's still five minutes away.

I want her to know she always has a place, one she doesn't have to work for, with me.

Our grocery bags beat against my thigh as we make the short trek from the store to the parking garage. Clouds have settled in close to the ground, leaning toward us like they have a secret to share. The first drop sprays my cheek while we're still on the sidewalk, and I smother my smile. The next one hits Cate, her blonde hair falling over her shoulder when she peeks up at me to see if I've noticed. I squeeze her hand and she returns it.

By the time we reach the crosswalk that leads to the garage, the irregular pitter-patter has climbed to a steady beat. Everyone else on the sidewalk rushes by us, seeking shelter, trying to open an umbrella overhead, covering themselves with bags or whatever random object they happen to be holding. But Cate and I don't hurry our steps. If anything, we slow our pace, remembering the last time we were caught together in a sudden storm.

For us, it's a good omen when it pours.

ACKnowLeDGemenTs

The idea for this book struck me like lightning and consumed me like smoke until I couldn't work on literally anything else until I got Cate and Paul's story out of my brain. I loved (almost) everything about writing it though, and I hope you, gracious reader, felt even just a hint of that spark while reading it. It was the fastest first draft I've ever written and possibly one of the most challenging stories to get right. I say that knowing I fully got it wrong the first go around.

With that, thank you to my wonderful beta readers for praising what I did well in the first draft (my ego requires it) and pointing out exactly where I missed the mark. This book is twenty times stronger because of your feedback.

And to my talented editor Alexandra: thank you for all your notes. Your critical eye and teacher's wisdom took this from a book that was pretty good to one I'm insanely proud of. Oh, and for not judging me for messing up blond vs. blonde after we just discussed this in my last novel. After all, I am but a mere mortal.

As you may have noticed, I dedicated this book to my mom. That was very intentional. Digging into Cate's character was one of the most difficult parts of writing this book, and I'm glad for it. Exploring the full depth of her sense of abandonment, brought on by neglectful parents, wasn't easy, because you're a great mom. You pulled double duty as a parent and never let me feel alone. For that, I thank you.

Last, and possibly most importantly, thank you to my wonderful husband Kelly. Your unwavering support of my author journey is the reason this book is possible. Thank you for carting my belongings to all my book signings, thank you for stepping in as an incredible dad when I need to disappear to write, and thank you for encouraging me to keep going, even when it's hard. Because sometimes it's really freaking hard. I love you.

ALSO BY RACHEL PLUCK

Are You In?
Are You Falling for It?
When It Pours

ABOUT THE AUTHOR

Rachel Pluck is the author of several contemporary romance novels and if it wasn't already obvious, she loves a good love story. Her entire life, she's been drawn to strong female protagonists staring down complex issues, and those are the types of stories she loves to create. In addition to being an author, Rachel is a marketing strategist living in southeastern Pennsylvania. When she's not obsessively reading, writing, or streaming old CW dramas (hello fellow TVD fans!) she can be found at home with her husband, wrangling their willful young daughter and three rescue pups.

Stay up to date with the author:
www.rachelpluckwrites.com
@rachelpluckwrites